Here Boy!

By Peter Belz

First Edition
Published By J&S Press
Lancaster, PA

ISBN: 979-8-9930895-4-6

Prologue

The dog had learned to be quiet.

Not because it was gentle, or obedient, or trained well. Quiet was just what kept things from getting worse. Noise invited attention. Attention invited hands. Hands did not mean help.

So the dog lay still in the dirt near the steps, breathing shallow, body folded tight around itself. The yard smelled wrong. The house smelled worse. Old anger. Old sweat. Something sour that never fully went away. These smells did not need names. They only meant danger.

The dog listened.

Footsteps came and went. Doors opened and closed. Sometimes there was shouting. Sometimes there was nothing at all, which was often worse. Silence meant waiting.

The fence sagged. One board was softer than the others, pushed inward at the bottom. Through that narrow gap, the dog could see a slice of the street. Shoes passed. Voices floated by. Lives moving somewhere else.

Most sounds didn't matter.

Then one did.

It wasn't loud. It wasn't close. It was different in a way the dog felt before it heard. A presence slowing. A rhythm changing. Something paying attention.

The dog lifted its head slightly.

There, on the other side of the fence, a figure had stopped.

The dog did not bark. It did not whine. It did not move forward. It had learned better than that. Instead, it let out a sound so thin it almost didn't exist. A sound meant for someone who knew how to listen.

For a long moment, nothing happened.

Then the air shifted.

The dog felt it first, a small loosening in its chest. A pause where there was usually none. The presence did not pass by. It stayed.

A voice came, low and careful. Not loud enough to carry. Not sharp enough to hurt.

The dog didn't understand the words.

It understood the tone.

For the first time in a long while, the sound it made back was not a warning.

It was a question.

And on the other side of the fence, something answered.

Chapter One – The Hit

The casting office sat on the third floor of a building that smelled like old carpet glue and the perspiration of thousands of failed auditions. Perry had been in rooms like this since he was thirteen, when he still believed that talent could overpower chance. At twenty-seven, he knew better, but here he was again, holding a flimsy sides sheet with dialogue written by someone who had probably never spoken to another human being.

The audition wasn't even for anything glamorous. A streaming show. Maybe. Possibly recurring. Definitely low budget pay, not even scale. But work was work, and he'd been slow for months. Barista wages were keeping him alive, but barely. He needed this one to go well.

He stepped into the room. The table of casting assistants didn't look up right away. Someone typed. Someone sighed. Someone whispered "go" without meeting his eyes.

He started the scene. It was supposed to be an argument. He tried to find the energy, the heat, the flicker of something alive in the lines. He took a step to the right for emphasis, the way he'd rehearsed, but his foot caught the edge of the taped mark on the floor. The stumble threw his balance off just enough that when he pivoted back, his shoulder clipped a tall LED light panel.

The panel wobbled. He reached for it. He missed.

The whole thing toppled and smacked him across the side of the head with a dull, plasticky thump. Not dramatic enough for a lawsuit, not soft enough to forget.

He saw a flash of white, then a wave of sound like someone had struck a tuning fork inside his skull.

"Are you okay?" one of the assistants asked, mostly out of liability rather than concern.

"I'm good," he said, because that's what actors say. You keep moving. You don't make trouble. You don't remind them you're made of meat and breakable things.

They made him sit down while someone brought over a clipboard with a waiver form that had probably been photocopied since the Clinton administration. He initialed where they told him. They let him finish the audition, which he did with the hollow detachment of a man pretending not to hear his heartbeat pounding in his ears.

When he finally stepped out into the hallway, the world felt brighter, louder, sharper. The elevator bell hit him like a slap. Someone laughing downstairs felt too close, as if the sound had been piped directly into his ears.

He told himself it was adrenaline. Embarrassment. A bad hit paired with a worse audition. Nothing more.

He pressed the elevator button again, and even the light click of it echoed in his skull.

He didn't know it yet, but the worst part wasn't the pain. It was the clarity.

The world had started talking to him, and it had no intention of whispering.

Chapter Two – Too Much Information

Perry's apartment had always been the kind of quiet that felt rented, not lived in. Tonight, the moment he unlocked the door, something about that quiet felt wrong. Too thin and breakable.

He dropped his bag on the floor and winced at the sound. It wasn't loud, but it cracked through the room and straight to his head. He froze, waiting for the ringing in his skull to settle, except it didn't. It then vibrated. A low, consistent thrum, like a heartbeat.

He breathed out slowly. "Stress," he told himself. "Just stress."

He turned on the kitchen light and jerked back when the bulb's hum flared sharp and sizzled. Had it always sounded like that? He'd lived here three years. Surely he would've noticed. But now it sounded like a swarm of insects behind glass.

He poured water into a glass, but before he took a sip, a smell drifted through the window. Not his smell. Someone else's. Roasted peppers, onions, garlic. The neighbor three floors down made that dish sometimes, but tonight it was as if she were sautéing vegetables on his countertop. He stepped back instinctively and almost laughed at himself, except the air really did feel thick with it.

"Concussion," he muttered. "Has to be."

He grabbed his phone to google symptoms, the way normal, responsible people do who ignore medical advice in favor of panic. But before he could type a single word, he heard something else: footsteps on the sidewalk outside. No big deal, except he could tell exactly how much the person weighed by the rhythm of their steps. He knew, for no reason he could explain, that they were carrying a plastic grocery bag. He could hear the faint shift of bottles knocking together.

He pressed his palms over his ears. It didn't help.

He walked to the window. A woman passed under the streetlamp, grocery bag in hand, the plastic flexing around two glass jars. He hadn't seen her before. But he'd heard her, impossibly.

He stepped back from the glass, abruptly.

This wasn't normal. This wasn't even close. His head throbbed with another vibration, deeper than the last, threading through the walls like a pulse. He tried to steady his breathing. Tried to pretend the apartment wasn't suddenly a living instrument tuned too tightly.

He made it to the couch and sat down slowly, gripping the cushion to feel something solid, something familiar. But even the fabric felt different under his hands, the texture sharper, every fiber had become an individual entity demanding attention.

"Okay," he whispered, because whispering felt safer. "This is temporary. Sleep will fix it."

He stretched out, closed his eyes, and waited for the dark to swallow the noise.

But even with the lights off, even with his eyes shut tight, he could still hear the distant buzz of the streetlamp outside. He could smell roasted peppers again, drifting up the vents. And somewhere in the building, water trickled through a pipe, steady as a metronome.

He lay there, afraid to move, afraid to breathe too deeply, afraid that the world had somehow shifted into high definition without asking him first.

Sleep didn't come.

Clarity did. Unwanted, uninvited, and far too sharp.

***

The morning crowd at the café was already buzzing when Perry walked in, which would've been fine any other day. Today it felt like stepping onto a battlefield where the weapons were voices, footsteps, and the shriek of the espresso grinder.

He blinked hard, trying to dull the edges of everything. No luck. The world stayed dialed up to eleven.

"Rough night?" Rina asked from behind the counter, tossing him an apron. She was the kind of coworker who always sounded two seconds from laughter. Normally he liked that. Today her voice came through like glass chimes.

"Didn't sleep much," he said, tying the apron strings. He kept his voice low, hoping the sound wouldn't ricochet off anyone's eardrums the way theirs were ricocheting off his.

Her eyes narrowed. "You look pale. Drink water."

He nodded, but the faucet's rattling pipes already echoed too sharply in his head. The sound from the pipes hit him with a weird, physical edge. He ignored it. Mostly.

The first customer approached. A guy in a suit, Bluetooth in his ear, eyes glued to his phone. "Medium drip," he mumbled.

Except Perry didn't just hear the words. He heard the residual tremor under them, the way people sound when they haven't eaten since yesterday and they're pretending they're fine. He caught the stale coffee smell on the man's clothes, the sour tang of anxiety on his breath.

Perry froze.

"Dude," Rina whispered, elbowing him. "He said medium drip."

He snapped back. "Right. Sorry."

He poured the coffee, handed it over, and forced a smile. The man didn't notice anything. Why would he? To him, Perry was just the guy behind the counter.

The next customer stepped up. A woman with a bright scarf and headphones around her neck. The lingering trace of vanilla shampoo hit Perry before she spoke, and he flinched at the clarity of it. She ordered a latte, but her tone carried something underneath it, something tight and brittle that told him she was fighting back tears even though her face didn't show it.

He made the latte quickly, trying to keep his hands steady. When he handed it to her, she gave him a polite smile and turned away. He felt her sadness trail behind her like a scent.

This was too much. Too intimate. Too invasive. He didn't want to know these things.

By noon, every click of a pen, every hiss of steaming milk, every shift of emotion in a customer's voice scraped over him like sandpaper. His chest felt tight. His breathing kept snagging. The room was too loud, too bright, too much of everything.

During a lull, he ducked into the alley behind the café. He leaned against the brick wall, letting the cold bite into his face.

"Get it together," he whispered. His breath fogged in the air. "Stop freaking out."

But how was he supposed to pretend this wasn't happening? That he wasn't hearing things he shouldn't, smelling things he shouldn't, sensing things he had no right to sense?

A car honked three blocks away, and he winced like it had exploded next to him.

He pressed the heels of his palms against his eyes until colors bloomed behind them. He waited for the world to settle.

It didn't.

But something else slid through the noise: a weak, soft whimper. Far away. Thin. Maybe a dog. Maybe in pain.

The sound threaded into him, sharper than everything else, and stayed.

He stood there staring at nothing, his heartbeat slow and heavy in his chest.

Trouble wasn't just happening to him.

It was calling to him.

Chapter Three – The Sound That Stayed

The whimper stayed with him all the way home. Not loud, not constant, just a sliver of sound that sank in the back of his mind and refused to let go. He tried to tell himself he was imagining it. His senses were shot, too sharp, too open. He didn't trust what they were doing anymore.

But when he turned down his block, the sound came again, soft, strained, unmistakable.

He slowed near the house with the sagging fence and patchy yard. He'd seen the dog there before, a small mutt with wiry fur and a skittish way of watching everything. Sometimes its water bowl was empty for days. Sometimes it paced the same dirt patch until the ground looked worn out.

Tonight, something felt different. He couldn't explain how he knew, just that he did.

He stepped toward the fence. The boards were soft with rot, pushing inward if he leaned too much. Through a narrow gap he saw the dog curled by the steps, body tight, shaking. Its breathing hitched every few seconds.

Then another sound drifted from inside the house. A dull thud. Followed by silence that felt worse than noise.

Perry seized up. He didn't hear the usual background clutter of a house, no TV, no footfalls, no dishes. Just that stillness and the dog's quiet, uneven breaths.

A smell seeped through the cracks in the wood. Whiskey. Sweat. Something tense, sour, unsettled. He also smelled, no, sensed something that ran right through him, it was unmistakable---fear. He didn't understand how he knew, but he did.

Perry stayed crouched there longer than he meant to. He didn't know what to do. He couldn't knock on the door. He couldn't pull the dog through the fence. He couldn't pretend he didn't hear or feel any of this either.

The dog lifted its head slightly, ears twitching at his presence. Its eyes looked dull in the darkness, tired in a way he recognized too well.

"It's okay," Perry whispered, barely audible.

Another thud inside. The dog flinched hard.

Adrenaline surged through him, quick and cold, leaving a tremor in his hands. He stepped back from the fence because he suddenly felt the urge to do something, anything, and he didn't trust himself not to push it too far.

The dog whimpered once more, a small sound that somehow landed heavier than anything else that day.

Perry walked the rest of the way home with his jaw clenched and his thoughts spinning. His awareness wasn't just picking up noise and smells anymore. They were pulling him toward things he couldn't ignore.

He didn't know what he was supposed to do. But he knew he couldn't leave things as they were.

***

By the next morning, Perry felt like he'd slept inside a speaker cabinet. Even small sounds left traces behind, as if they soaked into him instead of passing through. He walked into the café with his shoulders already tight, bracing for whatever the day was going to throw at him.

She was at the counter.

He noticed her first by the quiet she carried. Everyone else radiated something sharp or uneven, but she didn't. Her presence felt---steady. He couldn't explain that any more than he could explain anything else happening to him, but there it was.

Her name was Tess. She came in a few times a week. Usually early. Usually alone. She worked somewhere nearby, office job maybe, and she always ordered the same thing: small drip, splash of oat milk. She'd smile, say thanks, then disappear into the churn of morning commuters.

Today she was studying the pastry case quietly, taking her time the way she always did.

When she looked up and saw him, her face softened. "Hey. You're usually in earlier than this."

He shrugged, hoping his voice wouldn't betray how tightly wound he felt. "Rough night."

"Tell me about it," she said, but lightly, she wasn't trying to dig. Her tone carried a tiredness he wouldn't have caught before. Now he felt it immediately, just a small dip in the warmth of her voice, maybe a hint of something left unresolved from the night before.

It didn't overwhelm him. It actually calmed him.

"What can I get you?" he asked.

She hesitated, eyes drifting back to the pastries. "I'm torn. I should get something healthy. But I also didn't eat dinner last night, so---"

Before she finished the sentence, Perry felt a subtle pull of her attention toward the almond croissant. Not because she looked at it, but because something in her shifted. A small change in her breath, a quiet flicker of intention.

He reached in and picked it up.

"Oh," she said, surprised. "Yeah. That's exactly what I wanted."

He nodded, trying not to show how uncomfortable that made him. "Lucky guess."

"Lucky," she echoed, smiling.

Something about that smile cut through the morning noise. The grinders, the steam wand, the chatter, none of it hit him the way it had yesterday. Around her, the sharp edges dulled. His senses didn't overload. They didn't flare. They stilled.

He handed her the coffee. She wrapped her hands around the cup like she needed the warmth.

"You look exhausted," she said gently. "Are you alright?"

Perry opened his mouth, closed it again. He wasn't alright. He didn't know what he was. But he wasn't about to tell a near-stranger that the world had started screaming at him in ways previously unimaginable.

"Didn't sleep much," he said. "Nothing dramatic."

She studied him for a beat longer than usual. "Well, take care of yourself, okay?"

He nodded. "Yeah."

Tess walked out into the morning rush, and as soon as the door shut behind her, the café noise surged back in, bright, harsh, too much.

But for the brief minute she'd been there, everything felt manageable.

And that scared him more than anything.

16

Chapter Four – What He Could Hear

By the time Perry closed up the café that night, the city felt louder than it had any right to be. Every sound carried weight now. A bus braking a block away. Someone arguing faintly on a balcony. A metal gate rattling three storefronts down. It all pressed against him in ways he wasn't equipped to deal with.

He tried to walk home without letting his thoughts drift to the dog, but the memory of that thin, uneven whimper had already taken root. His perception worked against him. The closer he got to the house, the more tension he felt in the air.

He slowed as he reached the yard.

No sound at first. Just the usual scrape of branches, a distant car door, the muffled clatter of someone washing dishes nearby. Then he caught a scent he recognized too quickly: whiskey, stale and pungent. The same one from the night before.

He stepped toward the fence. The boards looked even weaker tonight, one of them bowed inward at the bottom as if something had pushed against it from the inside.

A muffled shout came from the house. Not loud, but abrupt. Then a door shut somewhere inside, quick and hard enough to make the dog flinch.

The house behind the fence fell still again, a kind of quiet that didn't feel natural.

Perry crouched near the fence, leaning close to the gap. The dog was there again, closer tonight, ribs shifting in quick, scared breaths. Even in the dim light, he could see a scrape on the dog's leg, the skin irritated and clearly left untreated.

The silence inside the house stretched on. Heavy. Unsettled.

Perry's pulse thudded at his temples. Instinct told him to move, to do something, to intervene. But another part of him, one conditioned by years of playing it safe, held him still. If he crossed the line now, there was no walking it back.

The dog shifted, inching toward the fence until its nose brushed the wood. A soft, tentative sound escaped it.

Perry swallowed. "I know," he whispered.

He didn't know why he said it. He just knew it was true.

He backed away before anyone inside could step out or spot him. He wasn't ready to confront anyone. He wasn't ready to explain why he was out here listening to things he shouldn't have been able to hear.

He walked home faster than he meant to, but the dog's breathing stayed with him, lodged on his shoulders, a weight he couldn't set down.

Inside his apartment, the quiet felt heavier than ever. Not comforting. Not safe. Just heavy.

He lay on the couch without turning on the lights, staring into the dark with his mind racing. Whatever was happening to him wasn't fading. If anything, it was becoming more defined, harder to ignore.

Someone was hurting that dog.
And pretending otherwise wasn't an option anymore.

***

He woke before sunrise, the apartment still dark, and for a moment he thought maybe the world had reset overnight. No pounding sounds, no sharp brightness, no stray emotions bleeding through from strangers. Just quiet.

Then a delivery truck braked at the end of the block, and the sound snapped through him. Not painful, just too clear. Too close.

So no. Nothing had reset.

He sat on the edge of the bed, hands pressed together. He needed to know what was happening to him. He needed to assess it somehow, even if he wasn't sure what he was looking for.

He stood in the kitchen and shut the refrigerator door gently, then a little harder. Both sounds landed with more detail than they should have, the rubber seal, the shift of the jars in the door. He turned on the faucet for a second, listening carefully. The rush of water didn't just sound loud; he could hear the slight variation in pitch when the pipes adjusted.

He shut it off. The silence felt thin.

He moved to the window and cracked it open. Air drifted in carrying scents he shouldn't have been able to pick apart: someone's laundry detergent from across the courtyard, the stale tang of yesterday's trash cans two buildings over, and beneath that, subtle but sharp, the dry, dusty smell of that dog's yard.

He closed the window quickly, breath tightening.

He sat on the couch and tried to slow his thoughts, but nothing stayed still. His sensitivity wasn't just heightened, it was tuned to things that had nothing to do with him, things he shouldn't know, feel, or smell.

He tried to focus just on his breathing. In. Out. Stay in the room. Stay present. Don't spin out.

But the world kept bleeding in.

A distant bus door hissing open.
Someone's alarm two floors up.
A bicycle chain clicking on the sidewalk.
Voices drifting muted from a radio in another
apartment.

None of it quiet. None of it ignorable.

He rubbed his eyes, palms against his face.

He wasn't losing his mind. This wasn't stress or
adrenaline or a concussion playing tricks. It was
something real. Something new. And the more he
tried to push it aside, the sharper it seemed to get.

He leaned back on the couch and let out a long
breath.

He couldn't tell anyone about this. Not yet. Not until
he understood it himself. He knew exactly what it
would sound like if he tried to explain: delusion,
overwhelmed, instability. He'd heard versions of that
tone plenty of times in his life. He wasn't inviting it in
now.

But one thing sat heavy in his chest, refusing to move.

He could hear suffering when it was close.
And now he knew where it lived.

He glanced toward the window, toward the direction of the yard.

He didn't know what he was going to do. But doing nothing already felt impossible.

Chapter Five – Selective Attention

Perry tried to make himself smaller.

Not physically. Internally.

He closed the blinds, shut the windows, and turned off the lights until the apartment felt sealed. He sat on the edge of the couch with his elbows on his knees and focused on the sound of his own breathing.

In.
Out.

If this was something he could control, this was where it would happen.

He listened.

At first, the room held. The refrigerator hummed. Pipes clicked once and settled. Nothing pressed in. Nothing demanded attention.

For a moment, he thought it had worked.

Then the layers returned.

A television murmuring three apartments over. Someone pacing upstairs, the rhythm uneven. A couple arguing quietly across the courtyard, words blurred but the tension unmistakable. Not loud. Just present.

Perry shut his eyes.

This wasn't like sight or sound anymore. It didn't arrive in fragments. It came intact, already carrying meaning, already telling him what mattered.

He tried to narrow it. Just one thing. The refrigerator. The steady hum. The predictability of it.

Behind it, something surfaced.

Fear.

Not his.

It moved through the building like a current, brief but unmistakable. Someone waking from a bad dream. Someone lying very still, hoping a door wouldn't open. Someone bracing for something they couldn't stop.

Perry's stomach tightened.

He stood and crossed the apartment, pressing his palms flat against the wall. The sensation faded, leaving quieter noise behind. But the awareness stayed.

This wasn't random.
And it wasn't receding.

If he responded to everything he sensed, he would never leave the apartment again. If he shut it out, he would have to live knowing he had felt something real and chosen to turn away.

Neither option felt sustainable.

He slid down the wall and sat on the floor, back against the chipped plaster. His heartbeat slowed. Not panic. Calculation.

Whatever this was, it wasn't asking for permission.

Tomorrow, and the next day, and the day after that, the world would keep offering him information he hadn't asked for.

At some point, soon, he would have to decide what kind of person that made him.

***

The next evening, the café was calm enough that Perry almost believed he could get through a shift without friction. He'd slept a little more, breathed a little slower, and kept his attention on manageable things: coffee orders, clean counters, the steady rhythm of people moving through the space.

Around seven, Tess walked in.

She wasn't in work clothes. Jeans, a colorful sweater, her hair pulled back. When she smiled at him, something in him eased before he had time to think about it.

"Off the clock?" he asked.

"Finally," she said. "Thought I'd grab a coffee and see if you wanted to walk out together when you're done."

"Yeah," he said, nodding before he fully caught up. "Sure."

She took the corner table and scrolled through her phone. He kept noticing her without trying to. Something in her posture looked tired, but eased. Like she'd finally let the day loosen its grip.

The bell over the door chimed. A couple came in, close together, voices low. Perry didn't need to hear what they were saying. The tension arrived intact. He pushed it aside and focused on Tess. Kept himself anchored.

They ordered coffees to go.

But his attention kept returning to Tess. Her breathing was slow and even. Her scent carried the cold air from outside. Each small movement sent a soft ripple through his awareness.

He didn't want this. Not like this. Not without control.

When his shift ended, he hung up his apron and joined her. They stepped out into the cooling evening.

"Long day?" he asked.

She exhaled. "You have no idea."

They walked side by side toward the corner. Traffic moved steadily. People passed in loose clusters. Perry tried to keep everything turned down, but the world slipped through anyway. A cyclist passed too close, the metal click of the gears sharp. A window opened overhead, and the smell of onions hit him as if he were standing in the kitchen.

He kept his eyes on the pavement.

"Perry," Tess said quietly. "You okay?"

He started to answer, then stopped.

Something shifted.

A car turning onto the street. The engine revved too hard. Tires scraped lightly against asphalt. Not loud.

But wrong. The speed. The line it was taking. The way it drifted closer to the curb than it should have.

And Tess stepped off the curb.

"Stop," Perry said.

She froze.

The car tore past, close enough that the wind of it brushed them.

Tess turned slowly, breath caught. "How did you know?"

Perry swallowed. He could lie. Shrug it off. Say he'd heard it coming.

Except he hadn't just heard it.

"I just did," he said.

She searched his face, then laughed softly, more relief than excitement. "You might have just saved my life."

The city hummed around them, every sound too precise. Perry felt the truth pushing up, insistent, waiting for space he wasn't ready to give it.

Tess met his eyes. "Thank you."

"You're welcome," he said, quieter than he meant to.

They stood there a moment longer, the street moving on around them, the space between what he knew and what he could say narrowing whether he liked it or not.

Chapter Six – The Same Direction

The next morning, Perry took a walk before work, hoping the movement would settle him. It didn't. The world felt stretched in the same strange way, sounds carrying farther than they should, scents cutting through the air even when he wasn't trying to notice them.

He paused at an intersection. A woman across the street was walking her dog, a thick-coated shepherd mix that padded calmly at her side. The leash stayed loose. The dog's ears kept shifting, catching things Perry couldn't hear. Or rather, things he used to not hear.

He froze.

He could hear them now.
Everything the dog reacted to, he could track too.

A car a block and a half away.
A gate clanking shut behind a building.
Someone dropping a bag of recycling down the

block.

The barely audible, quick rhythm of footsteps around the corner before the person even appeared.

The dog turned its head toward the sound at the exact same moment he did.

Perry's stomach tightened.

He forced himself to keep moving, but the thought chased him down the block anyway. He didn't want to compare himself to a dog. It sounded ridiculous, unhinged. But the more he walked, the more patterns he noticed. The way scents layered over each other. The way emotional tension carried in the air. The way his body responded before his mind had time to process anything.

It wasn't supernatural. It was sensory.

Animal, even.

He passed the neglected dog's house on the way back. No sound came from the yard, but he didn't need sound this time. The scent hit him immediately. Not strong, not foul, just wrong. A mix of fear, old dirt, dried sweat, something sharp he didn't want to identify. His body tightened in a way that had nothing to do with the abilities and everything to do with the dog behind that fence.

Perry stepped closer.
No movement. No whimpering.
But the smell lingered, heavy and stale.

He crouched near the fence again, pressing close to the same gap in the slats. The yard was empty. No dog on the steps. No sign of movement at all.

A cold ripple went through him.

His new senses weren't misfiring. They were warning him. The same way the shepherd on the street had reacted before noticing anything with its eyes.

He stood, feeling the weight of the realization settle in his chest.

Whatever had changed inside him wasn't random.
It wasn't chaos. It followed rules. Patterns. Instincts.

The kind that belonged to creatures who survived on awareness.
The kind that belonged to---dogs.

And now, standing at the fence of a dog that needed him, Perry realized something else too.

He wasn't helpless anymore.
Not if he learned how to use this.

He took one last breath near the fence, letting the scent settle into something he could follow if he needed to. Then he walked away with a new clarity he hadn't had before.

He didn't know the full shape of what he was becoming.
But he finally understood the direction of it.

***

Perry finished his shift in a fog, but not the overwhelmed kind from before. This was different. Sharper. More focused. Ever since watching the shepherd that morning and realizing how closely his own reactions mirrored it, something in him felt aligned in a way he didn't understand yet.

He stepped outside and headed home. He didn't rush. He didn't drift. He walked with a growing sense of purpose he hadn't had the day before.

Halfway down the block, a familiar scent moved across the breeze. Slight, but distinct enough to awaken something inside him, enough to pull him in a direction.

The dog's house was on the way.

He hadn't planned on stopping back tonight.
He just cared. Walking past the house without checking wasn't an option anymore.

When he reached the yard, the air carried more detail than the night before. The stale whiskey. The tension in the house. And beneath it, trace and uneven, the dog's scent. Alive. Weak. But alive.

Perry stepped toward the fence. He didn't crouch or strain to hear anything. He just let the information come the way it wanted to.

A gentle shift of weight inside the house.
A small scrape of claws against a floor.
A breath so faint he barely registered it, but steady enough to tell him the dog was conscious.

The dog wasn't in the yard tonight. It was lying somewhere on the other side of the door.

Perry let his perception settle. He didn't fight it this time. He didn't panic. He listened the way he had watched the shepherd listen that morning---still, open, alert.

The rhythm of the house shifted. A door inside slammed. He felt the vibration more than heard it, but nothing followed. The quiet returned, heavy but familiar.

He stepped away from the fence slowly. Not because he was overwhelmed. Not because he needed to escape. Because he understood exactly what the moment was:

Observation. Not reaction. Preparation.

On the walk back to his apartment, a car approached an intersection too fast. He heard the speed before the headlights rounded the corner. Without thinking, he paused on the sidewalk and waited as the car blew past.

He didn't flinch. He wasn't surprised. He had known.

It was the first moment that felt like control instead of chaos.

Back in his apartment, he didn't collapse onto the couch like before. He stood for a moment, absorbing what the night had revealed.

His mind wasn't spiraling.
It was sharpening.
And it was pointing him toward something he could no longer ignore.

Tomorrow, he'd be ready. For the dog.
For whatever came next.

Chapter Seven – Otis

Perry was sweeping the café floor when he caught something familiar on the air. Subtle at first. Warm.

Clean. A mild trace of the lotion Tess used on her hands. He froze mid-movement, the broom angled toward the floor.

She was close. Not inside. Not even on the block yet. But approaching.

Her scent grew clearer as it merged with the stale coffee and citrus cleaner that filled the shop at closing time. A moment later, the bell above the door chimed, exactly when he expected it to.

"Am I too late?" Tess asked.

He straightened the broom and tried not to look like he'd been waiting for her. "We're closed, technically. But I can let you in."

She stepped forward with a small smile, hands tucked into her jacket pockets. "Actually, I was hoping you might be closing up. Thought maybe we could walk together again."

He hesitated only long enough to make sure he was answering honestly. "Yeah. Let me lock up."

He shut off the lights, flipped the sign, and they stepped into the cool evening air. Their footsteps fell into an easy rhythm. Neither spoke for a few blocks. It was comfortable, the quiet sitting naturally between them.

Halfway home, something in Perry shifted. A signal. A pull. Not panic, just a feeling that told him the dog was troubled.

Perry slowed without thinking.

Tess noticed. "Everything okay?"

There's a dog I've been checking on. He isn't treated well, and I don't think he's doing alright tonight."

Tess studied his expression, not understanding but hearing the seriousness in his voice. "Alright. Lead the way."

They approached the fence, and Perry stopped. The air carried the dog's scent in thin, uneven threads. Weak breathing. Pain layered under fatigue. The impressions pushed against Perry's awareness, not as words but as something close to intention.

He crouched near the familiar gap in the slats. Tess knelt beside him. In the dim porch light across the yard, he didn't appear. But Perry felt him.

He whispered, "He's in there."

As if in response, a small, exhausted dog struggled across the yard. Tess covered her mouth. "That's awful, look at him, he's in bad shape"

Perry's voice was steady. "I can't leave him like this."

Tess looked around the yard, then back at him. "Perry, we can't just take someone's dog."

"He's not someone's dog," Perry said quietly. "Not in any way that matters."

She hesitated, torn. The dog let out a painful sigh. It erased whatever was left of her uncertainty.

"Alright," she said. "What do we do?"

Perry tested the bottom slat of the fence. The wood was flimsy from rot, bending easily under his fingers. He looked at her. "Help me lift it. Just enough for him to crawl through."

Together they shifted their weight and pulled upward. The wood groaned softly as it rose a few inches. Enough.

Perry leaned forward. "Otis. Come here."

Tess looked at him. "Otis?"

"I don't know how I know," Perry whispered. "I just do."

A pause. A thread of recognition. Then movement.

Otis emerged from the yard, limping. His ribs showed beneath his wiry fur. The scrape on his leg was worse, irritated and swollen. He dragged himself closer to the gap, eyes fixed on Perry with a weary, desperate clarity.

Tess's voice cracked. "He's just a baby---"

Perry slid a hand under the lifted slat, palm open and steady. "Come on, Otis. You're okay now."

Otis hesitated only a moment before pushing himself forward, trembling as he squeezed under the fence. Tess reached out and supported him as his back legs cleared the wood.

The instant Otis was free, a surge of relief passed through Perry. Not his own. Otis's. A quiet wave of recognition and trust.

Tess felt something shift too, not in sensation but in understanding. She looked at Perry in a new way, with a gentler, steadier gaze.

"Where do we take him?" she asked.

"My place," Perry said. "It's close. We'll figure everything else out later."

Tess nodded. "Then let's get him there."

Perry gathered Otis carefully into his arms. The dog's head dropped against his chest, settling there with a kind of exhausted certainty. Tess stepped in beside him, ready to help in any way she could.

Together, the three of them walked away from that yard, leaving the broken fence and empty house behind.

The night felt different now. Not lighter. But aligned. As if the path ahead had been waiting for this exact moment.

***

Perry lived on the third floor of a narrow walk-up. The stairs were steep, uneven in places, and dimly lit by a single bulb that flickered whenever someone shut a door on the lower floors. He carried Otis carefully, feeling every shift in the dog's breathing as they climbed. Tess walked close behind, ready to steady them if needed.

At the top of the stairs, Perry unlocked his door and pushed it open with his shoulder. The apartment was small, even for the city. A single living room fed straight into a galley kitchen. One short hallway led to the bedroom, its door half-open. Everything had the worn, practical look of a place someone lived in because it was all they could afford, not because it inspired them.

He stepped inside and crossed the living room in a few quick strides. An old, folded blanket waited near the couch, the warmest corner of the apartment, a spot for Otis to lie down comfortably. Perry lowered him there with care.

Otis exhaled, a soft, shaky sound that settled the room.

Tess knelt beside him. "Poor thing."

Perry crouched on the other side. The apartment felt different now. Smaller, but in a way that made sense. Otis's presence filled the space, his scent, his warmth, the fragile rhythm of his breathing. And underneath it all, Perry felt the hazy impressions again, the subtle emotional shifts that weren't his.

Recognition. Safety.
A kind of relief that hit deeper than sound.

Tess reached a hand toward Otis, then paused and looked at Perry.

"Go ahead," Perry said quietly.

She touched Otis's back. The dog didn't flinch. He simply rested, settling into the blanket, it was the first real comfort he'd had in days.

Perry stood and stepped into the kitchen. He filled a bowl with water and set it on the floor. Otis lifted his head, drank a few careful laps, then rested again.

"He needs a vet," Tess said softly.

"I know," Perry said. "But I can't take him anywhere tonight. He wouldn't make it far."

"We'll figure it out tomorrow."

He nodded.

A quiet came to rest over the apartment, the kind that wasn't awkward or tense. It was just there, the three of them sharing the same tight space with the same exhausted purpose. Tess looked around and then back at Perry, something unspoken in her expression.

"You didn't hesitate," she said. "Back in the yard."

"He needed help."

Perry met her eyes.

"You knew you were coming home with Otis tonight," she said.

He didn't have a simple answer. He didn't try to offer one.

Tess didn't push further. She just nodded, accepting there was more happening than he was ready to explain.

Otis shifted weakly on the blanket, and Perry felt the echo of it inside himself. A calm impression, not language, not thought, just a feeling that mattered.

Tess stood slowly. "I can stay a little longer if you want help watching him."

Perry shook his head. "You've done enough. Get home before it gets too late."

She hesitated, then nodded. "Text me if anything changes."

"I will, and thank you."

She slipped her jacket on and let herself out quietly.

The apartment sank into stillness again. Perry sat on the floor beside Otis, not touching him, just close. The dog lifted his head a fraction and gave a delicate breath, something like gratitude, something like trust.

Perry felt it settle through him.

Home.

Whether the impression came from Otis or from Perry himself didn't matter.

For the first time, they were safe in the same place.

Chapter Eight - Staying

Perry opened the café alone that morning. The gate rattled as he pulled it up, louder than usual, or maybe he was just too tired to brace for the noise. He hadn't slept. Otis had shifted in and out of shallow rest all night, and every feeble breath, every twitch of discomfort had kept Perry alert, checking on him, offering water, adjusting the blanket.

The apartment smelled like Otis when Perry left. It comforted him.

He moved through the opening routine in a haze. Turn on the lights. Grind the beans. Stack the cups. Somewhere between wiping down the counter and checking the pastry case, his phone buzzed.
Mom.

He considered ignoring it, but that never worked. He answered on the second ring.

"Hey, Mom."

"You sound tired. Everything alright?"

"I'm good," he said. "Just opening up. Early day."

"Are you eating enough? You don't sound like you're eating enough."

"Everything's great, Mom. Really. I'm working now. Gotta go, talk later."

He hung up gently before she could find the thread of a longer conversation. He loved her, but he didn't have the energy to lie convincingly this morning.

The door swung open behind him. Rina stepped in, coat half buttoned, hair in a messy bun.

"You look like stale bread," she said. "Like, the butt end no one wants."

"Thanks. Really uplifting."

She took a closer look at him. "What happened to you?"

"I had a long night," he said, hoping that would be enough.

It wasn't.

She angled her head. "You look like you didn't sleep at all."

He didn't answer.

Rina didn't push. She never did. She just grabbed an apron and tied it on, giving him space to exist in whatever mood he came in with.

After an hour of steady customers, Perry leaned against the counter, rubbing his eyes. The clock above the pastry case seemed louder than usual. Every click of the second hand felt like it was drilling into his brain.

Rina glanced over. "You want to take your break early?"

"I actually need to ask you something," Perry said. "Could I maybe head out after the lunch rush? I have an audition."

The lie dropped out of his mouth smoother than it should have.

Rina sighed. "If you're asking whether I can cover the last few hours, sure. But you better book a role this time. Or at least bring me back a bagel."

"Thanks," he said quietly.

She gave him a softer look. "Whatever's going on, take care of yourself."

He nodded.

His phone buzzed again. He checked the screen.

Tess.

He stepped into the back hallway to answer. "Hey."

"How's Otis?" she asked. No small talk, just straight to the thing that mattered.

"He made it through the night," Perry said. "But he needs a vet. I'm leaving work early to take him."

"I'm coming," Tess said.

"You don't have to. It's gonna be a long day."

"I know," she said. "I'm still coming. Text me when you're on your way home."

"Alright," he said. "I'll meet you halfway."

"Good."

They hung up without anything extra. It wasn't abrupt. It was just the tone of people who didn't need filler words anymore.

Perry slipped the phone into his pocket and leaned against the wall for a moment. The exhaustion worked its way deeper. But underneath it, something steadier held him up.

He wasn't doing this alone.

Two hours later, Rina waved him off with a half-hearted salute. "If you pass out on the subway, I'm not picking you up."

"I'll keep that in mind."

He left the café and stepped into the early afternoon light. His whole body wanted sleep, but the pull toward helping Otis was stronger.

Tess was already waiting at the corner a few blocks away, hands in her coat pockets, watching for him.

"Ready?" she asked as he approached.

He nodded.

They started toward his apartment together, the same pace, the same purpose.

***

The walk back to Perry's apartment felt longer than usual. Not because of the distance, but because Perry kept feeling faint impressions from Otis, small pulses of discomfort, a wrinkle here and there, the dog's patience wearing thin. Tess could tell something was off with Perry, but she didn't press. She matched his pace quietly.

Inside the apartment, the air was warm and smelled of an old pizza box, a weeks' worth of dirty laundry, and Otis. Otis lifted his head weakly when they entered, eyes finding Perry first, then Tess. His tail didn't move, but a fragile exhale slipped out, something close to relief.

Tess knelt beside him. "He looks worse today."

"He is," Perry said. "He barely drank any water this morning."

Perry crouched next to them, close but not touching. He didn't need contact to feel the impression carried outward from Otis, thin but present. Pain. Fatigue. But underneath all of it, trust.

Tess looked up. "We can't wait anymore."

"I know."

They wrapped Otis in the blanket he'd slept on overnight. Perry lifted him carefully, and Otis didn't resist. Tess held the door open, staying close without interfering.

They called an Uber because Perry didn't have the strength for another long carry. The driver muttered something sympathetic about the dog, then focused on the road. No questions.

At the vet's office, the tech at the front desk took one look at Otis and ushered them straight back. No paperwork. No waiting room. Just urgency.

The exam room was too bright under the fluorescent lights. The vet entered moments later, calm and practiced.

"What do we have here?" she asked, kneeling beside Otis.

Perry watched every movement. Each time Otis tensed, Perry felt it echo slightly in his own body. Tess noticed him wince once or twice, but didn't call attention to it.

"He's dehydrated," the vet said. "Malnourished. Infection starting in that leg. He's lucky someone brought him in today."

Tess let out a quiet breath. Perry's jaw tightened.

"We'll need to run tests," the vet continued. "Start fluids. Antibiotics. Pain management."

"Do whatever he needs," Perry said.

The vet nodded and stepped out, leaving them in the cold, bright quiet.

Otis shifted on the table. The movement was slight, but the impression that followed wasn't. It hit Perry with surprising clarity. A mild pressure in his chest. Not fear. Not pain.

Just presence. A single, unmistakable feeling.

Here.

Perry froze.

The impression didn't form a word, not really, but it carried the shape of one. A clear announcement of existence, directed straight at him.

Tess noticed the way his expression changed. "Perry? What is it?"

He swallowed. "He knows he's safe."

It was the only explanation he could offer without sounding unhinged.

A moment later, another impression washed through him. Relief this time. Warm, softened, and unmistakably Otis's. The dog wasn't calling for help anymore. He wasn't searching. He was simply connected.

The vet returned with medicines. She placed the IV carefully, started fluids, administered medication. Otis relaxed under her hands, breathing more evenly as the pain eased.

"He'll need to stay for a few hours," she said. "You can wait here if you like."

When she left again, Tess and Perry settled on the small bench along the wall. Their shoulders didn't touch, but they sat close enough that Perry felt steadier.

Tess looked at him gently. "You're doing the right thing."

Perry stared at Otis. "Feels like I've known him longer than a day."

Tess smiled and said, "Some dogs choose their person right away. They don't need time."

Perry rubbed the back of his neck. "I told Rina I was leaving for an audition."

Tess nodded. "So she wouldn't ask questions."

"Yeah."

"That's not lying," she said. "That's surviving."

Perry exhaled, exhaustion finally catching up to him.

They stayed like that in the quiet for a while. Otis rested on the table, breathing evenly under the medication, the quiet thread between him and Perry holding steady and sure.

The silence wasn't heavy.

It was honest.

Chapter Nine – No Pet Policy

They waited at the vet for nearly three hours. Otis slept under the medication, every so often letting out a small sigh that made Perry's stomach turn. He'd been awake for almost twenty-four hours, and every minute was catching up with him. He sat hunched forward on the bench, head in his hands, eyes drifting between Otis and the floor.

Tess stayed beside him. She didn't ask questions. She didn't try to fill the silence. She just kept her coat on, and her hands folded in her lap, glancing at Otis every now and then, willing time to move faster.

When the vet finally came back in, she spoke with a calm certainty that Perry clung to.

"He's stable," she said. "Hydrated. Responding to antibiotics. He's still weak, but he can go home with you today."

Perry nodded, a wave of relief washing through him. Tess let out a quiet breath of her own.

"We'll send you with medications and instructions," the vet added. "He'll need rest. Gentle meals. Keep the leg clean."

"We can do that," Perry said.

The tech returned with discharge papers and a small bag of supplies. Perry helped wrap Otis in the blanket again. Tess lifted a corner without being asked.

Outside, the early evening air felt cold and flat, but Otis breathed easier than before. They walked instead of calling another Uber, taking slow steps down the sidewalk.

Tess watched Perry carefully. "You're exhausted."

"I didn't sleep."

"I figured." Her voice stayed soft, not prying. "You've been carrying him through all of this. Anyone would look wrecked."

Perry shifted Otis in his arms. "He's worth it."

She nodded, her expression warming. "I agree."

They kept walking, the city easing into a quieter hour. A bus hissed as it pulled to the curb. Someone argued on a fire escape above them. Perry seemed to notice everything and nothing at once, his attention tethered to the dog breathing weakly against his chest.

"You know," Tess said quietly, "most people wouldn't have done this."

"Done what?"

"Taken responsibility for a dog they met yesterday. Stayed up all night. Brought him to a vet. Paid for it. All of it."

Perry shook his head. "I couldn't leave him there."

"I'm not saying you should have," she said. "I'm saying it says something about you."

He didn't know how to answer that. He just kept walking.

When they reached his building, Tess unlocked the downstairs door for him so he wouldn't have to juggle Otis. She stayed close behind as they climbed the stairs slowly, step by step.

In the apartment, Perry set Otis gently onto the same blanket in the corner of the living room. Tess knelt beside him, brushing some loose fur from his head.

"He already looks better, safer," she said.

"He is," Perry answered quietly.

Tess looked up at him. Dark circles carved deep under his eyes. His shoulders slumped. But there was something steady in him too, something she wasn't used to seeing in people who were stretched thin.

"I don't know how you're holding it together," she said.

"I'm not sure I am."

"That's fair."

She stood, brushing her hands off. "I'll give you a little space. You both need rest. Text me later and let me know how he's doing."

"I will."

She hesitated for a moment at the door. Not because of confusion or apprehension, just concern.

"You did a good thing today," she said.

Then she left, stepping quietly into the hallway.

The apartment set into stillness. Perry sat on the floor beside Otis again, close. The dog shifted, breathing easier now, head settling into the blanket. Perry let out a long breath of his own.

Not a connection moment.
Not an emotional surge.
Just the quiet relief of two living beings finally in a place where they weren't suffering.

For now, that was enough.

***

Perry slept for the first time in almost a full day. It wasn't planned. He sat down on the floor next to Otis, leaned back against the couch for a second, and his body shut down. When he woke again, the room was dimmer, the light outside an early-evening gray. His back ached from the angle he'd collapsed in.

Otis was awake. Quiet, but alert. His eyes tracked Perry before his head moved, and Perry felt a soft, steady presence from him. Not a signal, not a word. Just awareness. The apartment felt warmer for it.

Perry rubbed his face and stood, stiff from the floor. He filled a bowl with water and brought it to the blanket. Otis stretched his nose toward it, drank a little, then quieted again.

There was a sound in the hallway. Footsteps. Slow ones. Perry looked toward the door before the knock came, a dim prickle of instinct telling him someone was coming. He didn't question it.

A moment later, a few taps.

"Mr. Heller?"

Perry tensed. The landlord.

He glanced at Otis. The dog's ears dipped, a quiet unease settling around him.

Perry cracked the door open. The landlord stood in the hallway in a heavy coat, brief case in hand.

"Evening," the landlord said. "Everything alright in here?"

"Yeah," Perry said, blocking the view into the apartment.

"Had a complaint earlier. Someone thought they saw a dog. You know the pet policy."

Perry swallowed. "No dog here."

The landlord nodded like he half believed him, half didn't. He didn't push inside. He didn't ask to look. He just stood there, taking in the smell of the apartment, the tiredness in Perry's face.

When the door shut, Perry let out a breath he didn't realize he'd been holding. He stood still a moment, hand on the lock, mind racing. Losing Otis wasn't an option, not now that the dog was finally safe. Not after everything he'd seen in that yard.

Otis watched him from the blanket, eyes steady. A faint impression reached Perry. Not fear exactly. More like a question. As if the dog was trying to understand whether Perry was staying with him.

There was another sound from the hallway. Different footsteps. Lighter. Familiar. Before the knock even landed, Perry knew it was Tess.

He opened the door before she could knock again.

"Oh," she said. "Hi. I didn't know if you'd be up."

"I'm up," Perry said. His voice still rough from sleep.

Tess stepped inside, taking in the dim apartment and the blanket where Otis lay. She moved straight to the dog and knelt beside him.

"He looks a little better," she said.

"He drank some water."

"Good."

Perry watched the two of them together, feeling a rush of warmth come over him.

Tess looked back at him. "You look like someone unplugged you and plugged you back in."

"I slept."

"That's progress."

Her eyes drifted toward the door, like she'd caught a leftover tension in the air. "Everything alright? You opened the door fast."

"Landlord stopped by," Perry said. "Someone said they saw a dog."

Tess's expression shifted slightly. "Meaning you--- Otis?."

"Probably."

"No pet policy?"

"Exactly."

She didn't react with fear or worry, just understanding. Her hand rested lightly on Otis's side.

"It'll be alright," she said quietly.

Perry nodded, but his mind was already replaying the landlord's face, the tone, the pause in the hallway. The feeling he'd had before the knock. The way Otis responded to it.

Pressure building from both directions.

He leaned against the counter, arms crossed, watching Tess stroke Otis's fur. The apartment felt too small.

Tess looked up at him again, softer this time. "You don't have to do this alone."

He didn't answer. He wasn't sure he could without cracking something open.

Outside, footsteps passed in the hallway again. Normal ones. Someone going to their own apartment. Perry heard them clearly, more clearly than he should have, and he shut his eyes for a second, steadying himself.

When he opened them, Tess was still watching him.

Not suspicious. Not worried. Just present.

The rope began to pull on both ends.

Chapter Ten – Found

Two weeks passed. Otis healed with a speed that surprised everyone except Otis. The limp was nearly gone. His eyes were brighter. He explored the apartment like he had lived there his whole life, tracking Perry from room to room with a confidence that made the first week feel distant.

Perry fixed into a new rhythm too. His awareness was still sharp, sometimes too sharp, but he had learned how to live with it and to lean on it when needed. City noise no longer crashed into him. Smells separated cleanly without overwhelming him. The impressions he felt from Otis were clearer now, almost conversational. He still kept all of it to himself.

Tess slipped into the edges of their routine in an easy, natural way. She stopped by when she was in the neighborhood. She joined them on walks. She checked on Otis without hovering and checked on Perry without calling it that. It was steady and subtle, which he appreciated more than he ever said out loud.

That morning, she had texted early saying she would be running errands near the café and might stop in later. Perry fed Otis, scratched his head, and headed out for the early shift.

The air was cool and sharp. Perry could separate each scent along the sidewalk as he walked. Fresh dough from the bakery. Damp concrete. A woman's perfume that drifted toward him in a straight trail. Nothing alarming, just information, all of it quiet enough to manage.

He unlocked the café, flipped on the lights, and started the opening routine. Rina came in a little while later, rubbing sleep from her eyes.

"You look human today," she said. "Big improvement."

"Thanks," Perry said. "Otis is doing better."

"Good. You should bring him in sometime."

"He's not a coffee shop dog."

"Every dog is a coffee shop dog if you let them be," she said, already halfway to the pastry fridge.

She stopped.

There was a sheet of paper taped to the front window. Something neither of them had put there. Something Perry hadn't noticed when he walked in.

Rina peeled it off the glass.

"Hey," she said. "Is this your dog?"

Perry looked at the paper. His stomach tightened.

A missing-dog flyer. Cheap printer paper. Blurry photo. But unmistakable.

Otis. Looking thin. Neglected. The way he had looked the night Perry found him.

Across the top, in heavy black letters:

Lost Dog: Otis

A description sat below the photo. Age. Coloring. Last seen. A phone number, but no name.

Rina held it toward him. "Weird timing, right. You adopt a dog named Otis and now someone is looking for one. Is that a coincidence." More of a statement than a question.

Perry took the flyer from her. His fingers felt colder than they should.

"I don't know."

"You should call the number," she said. "If it is a different dog, no big deal. If it is him, maybe someone misses him."

Perry did not answer. His awareness was searching without him even trying. There was a scent clinging to the flyer, barely there but familiar. Something sharp beneath the ink and paper. Something menacing. Something he recognized from the yard where he had found Otis.

Pain. Fear. Rotting fence wood. A hint of whatever lingered in that house.

A scent Otis had never forgotten.

Rina was still talking but her voice faded into the background. Perry folded the flyer once and slipped it into his jacket pocket.

"You good?," she asked.

"Yeah," Perry said. "Just thinking---and hungry."

"Eat something before you pass out on the espresso machine."

She headed to the back room.

Perry leaned against the counter for a moment. The café felt too bright now. Too exposed.

His phone buzzed. A message from Tess.

I will be near the café soon. Want to walk home later.

Perry stared at the screen for a second before typing.

Yes.

He slid the phone into his pocket and steadied his breathing. Otis had been safe for two weeks. Healing. Growing stronger.

But someone had been close enough to tape that flyer to the window. Someone was looking. Someone who wanted him back.

The quiet part of their story had ended.

***

Tess picked Perry up after work. She waved through the l window, casual as always, unaware of the folded flyer burning a hole in his jacket pocket. He closed the café door behind him and they started on.

"You alright?," she asked.

"Yeah," he said. "Long shift."

She didn't buy it, but she let it slide as they made their way to Perry's apartment.

The apartment was dim when they arrived. Otis stood as soon as the door opened, tail slow but steady, greeting Perry with that familiar weight of recognition. Perry knelt to scratch behind his ears. The calm that usually came with that moment didn't.

Otis noticed.

He nudged Perry's shoulder, then stepped back, sensing something he could not see.

Tess closed the door behind them. "He looks good," she said. "Better every day."

"Yeah."

Perry reached into his pocket. He hesitated. Then he unfolded the flyer and set it on the coffee table. Otis froze the moment the paper touched the wood.

His body went rigid. His ears flattened. A deep tremor moved through him, not loud, not dramatic, but unmistakable. He stepped forward cautiously, nose hovering over the page. The scent hit him and he recoiled, a low whine slipping out before he could stop it.

Perry felt the impression slam into him like a cold air in his lungs.

The scent. The house. The hands that had grabbed him. The place he had wanted to escape. Danger.

Tess stepped closer. "Perry. What is that?"

He couldn't minimize it. Not with Otis shaking beside him. Not with the air in the room compressing.

"It was taped to the café window this morning," he said quietly. "They're looking for him."

Tess ran her fingers along the edge of the paper, just once. She didn't pick it up. "Someone who was close enough to put this where you could see it."

"Yeah, a coincidence that's too close for comfort."

Otis pressed against Perry's leg, sending a hard pulse of fear that Perry couldn't ignore. It wasn't the sharp panic from the night he rescued him. It was focused. Specific. About a person. About a memory.

Tess watched him. "This is not just a lost dog situation."

"No," Perry said. "It is not."

She crouched beside Otis and held out her hand. He leaned into her slowly, shaking less with each breath. She stayed there with him until the tension in his body eased.

Then she looked at Perry. "We need to decide what to do next."

Perry nodded, even though he had no plan, even though his body felt tight with a mix of instinct and dread he could not name.

Otis nudged the flyer with his paw as if pushing it away from himself. The message was clearer than anything Perry had felt so far.

Not safe.

Perry swallowed hard. "Yeah," he said. "We do."

Chapter Eleven – Flight Response

Perry and Tess walked Otis after sunset, drifting through one of the quieter routes they'd resolved into over the past few weeks. Otis moved confidently, tail flicking as he sniffed along the sidewalk. Everything about the night felt routine.

A car eased down the street toward them. Nothing unusual.

Until the driver looked out his window, saw Otis, and everything in him snapped into recognition.

Brakes screamed. The car jerked sideways. The door flew open.

"HEY! THAT'S MY DOG!"

Otis recoiled, muscles bunching. Tess jerked the leash back in pure reflex.

"Run!," Perry said.

They took off.

The man sprinted after them, shouting, footsteps hammering the pavement. Tess ran hard, Otis flying beside her.

At the next block, she veered left on instinct. Perry grabbed her arm and yanked her sharply the other way, just as two people stepped out of a doorway she would've collided with full force. She didn't have time to question it; she just ran.

A cyclist shot out from behind a parked van, silent, sudden, impossible to predict. Perry had already guided her out of its path before she even saw it.

Her breath caught, but there was no space for words.

At the intersection ahead, she saw no headlights, no noise, nothing. She started to step out.

Perry slammed an arm across her chest.

A delivery truck blasted through the cross street at highway speed.

Tess stumbled back, heart climbing her throat. Still, she kept moving when Perry pulled her along. They tore down a narrow alley, Otis right at Perry's side.

The man's voice finally faded into the distance.

Only then did they slow.
Only then did their lungs start catching up.

Otis leaned against Perry's leg, panting lightly. Tess braced a hand on the brick wall, pulling in deep breaths. The adrenaline began to drain, and in its place came everything she hadn't had time to process.

She turned to Perry sharply.

"What was that?" Her voice was thin but firm. "Perry, that wasn't just lucky. You moved before anything happened. You pulled me out of the way of people I couldn't even see. You dodged a cyclist who didn't make a sound. You stopped me before a truck came that I swear wasn't anywhere near us."

Perry blinked. "I was just trying to get us away."

"That's not what I'm saying." She stepped closer, breath still uneven. "You reacted to things no normal person could've known were coming. You didn't even look half the time. You just, moved."

Perry swallowed hard. The alley felt too quiet now.

Tess didn't soften the question.

"Perry. What's going on with you?"

He finally met her eyes.

67

"I don't know how to explain it," he said quietly. "But, I'll try."

Otis nudged his leg, steady and certain, as if stealing the moment between them.

***

The alley behind them still carried the tension of the chase, and the man's shouting echoed faintly in memory even though the street was quiet now. Otis stood slightly ahead of Perry and Tess, watching the entrance to the alley with a steady posture, alert but controlled. Tess's breathing was still uneven from the run.

"Which way?," Tess whispered.

Perry listened. A single engine on a nearby block. A slow change in its movement. A pause that did not match normal traffic.

"Left," he said. "Avoid the main road."

Tess nodded. They moved quickly along the side street. Otis walked in front, checking their path, occasionally glancing back to make sure Perry and Tess were with him. Perry stayed close behind him, reading the sounds in the distance.

Halfway down the block Perry stopped.

Tess halted beside him. "What is it?"

Perry listened again. "He is turning toward us."

Tess's eyes narrowed. "How do you know?"

"I do."

She accepted it without pushing.

Perry guided her between two parked cars. Otis slipped through first, already focused on the darker space beyond. They crossed into a side yard and stilled behind a row of trash bins, low enough to stay hidden but ready to move.

A car rolled slowly onto the next street. The man leaned out the window, scanning the sidewalks. His voice carried echoing as he called Otis's name.

Otis's stance shifted. Not fear. Readiness. He watched every movement of the car, muscles set and waiting for a cue. The moment brought something out in him. He was now protecting what he loved most.

The car paused at the corner. The man shouted again. Then the engine tone changed and the vehicle moved away.

Perry waited a few seconds longer, listening.

"He is heading toward the next street," Perry said.

Tess let out a slow breath. "How did you know he was close before we saw the car?"

"I heard the tires on gravel at the turn," Perry said. "And the vibration under the pavement when he slowed."

Tess stared at him. The confusion in her expression was hard and clear.

"No one hears things like that."

Perry met her eyes. "I do."

Otis shifted his weight, watching both of them, ready for the next move.

"We go now," Perry said. "This block is clear."

They crossed the yard and climbed a low retaining wall. Perry led them through a string of backyards and narrow service alleys where the noise of the street faded. Otis moved ahead, checking corners before they reached them, glancing back only when he needed confirmation.

A few minutes later they reached Perry's building. Perry scanned the area one more time, listening for any sign of the car. Nothing.

Inside the stairwell Tess finally stopped him.

"Perry," she said. "Tell me what is going on with you."

He looked at her. No deflection left. "I know."

Otis waited at the bottom step, watching both of them without tension.

Perry nodded. "I will."

They continued up toward the apartment.

Chapter Twelve – What He Told Her

Inside the apartment Perry locked the door and checked it again. Tess stayed a few steps away, giving him space but watching his posture. Otis walked a steady path around the room, then stopped near the hallway where he could track both Perry and the entrance.

Perry's phone buzzed.

His mother.

He answered on instinct. "I'm okay," he said. "I'll call you tomorrow." He kept it short and ended the call before she could ask anything else.

Another notification appeared.
Email from his agent.

Tess glanced at it. "Is that work?"

"Self-tape," Perry said. "Tomorrow."

"You should do it," Tess said. Her voice was quiet and even.

Perry put the phone face down on the counter.

Tess stepped a little closer. "Perry. We need to talk."

He didn't respond.

"You don't have to give me everything at once," she said. "Just start with something."

He let out a breath. "You saw what happened."

"I saw enough to know you weren't guessing," Tess said. "And I saw you react to things before I had any reason to."

Perry nodded once.

Tess softened her tone. "How did you do it, how did you know?."

"It's hard to explain."

"Well try, how long have you been so---."

"Since I hit my head."

She straightened slightly. "So it started after that accident you told me about?."

"Yes," he said. "Not all at once. It built up. Little things first. Then more. It kept getting stronger."

Tess considered him for a moment. "And what exactly is happening to you? Not what you think. What you know."

Perry sat down at the table, finally settling in a way that showed how long he had been holding this in.

"My senses changed," he said. "Not in a normal way. I hear things I shouldn't. I smell things before they're close. I pick up patterns I shouldn't be able to. It's not instinct. It's not training. It's just there."

Tess sat across from him. "And you're certain it started after the injury?"

"Yes."

"Has anything ever made it stop or slow down?"

"No."

"And you didn't tell anyone?"

Perry shook his head. "Who would I tell? How do you say something like that without sounding as if you need help?"

Tess didn't disagree. She watched him carefully, not alarmed but processing the information.

"Tonight," she said, "you weren't surprised by anything. You reacted before things were visible or audible. That's incredible---but strange."

"I know," Perry said. "And it's been getting more precise."

"Does it hurt?" she asked.

"No."

"Does it overwhelm you?"

"Sometimes," he said. "When it spikes without warning."

Tess leaned forward slightly. "Can you control it?"

"Not fully," Perry said. "But I am getting better at it."

Otis sat near them, alert and listening.

Tess nodded slowly. "Then tell me everything from the moment you hit your head. Every detail. Anything that felt different."

Perry held her gaze.

"I will," he said.

And he began.

***

They stayed on the couch after the conversation ended. Not talking. Not avoiding each other. Just letting the night settle around them. Otis shifted onto his side near the doorway, eyes half-open, relaxed for the first time since they got home.

Tess glanced at Perry. "Are you alright?"

"Yeah," he said. "I think so."

She studied him for a moment longer. Something in her face had changed since the alley. It wasn't softness. It was clarity. Decision.

"You didn't have to tell me everything," she said. "But you did."

"I trust you," Perry said.

Tess nodded once, like she had needed to hear it spoken out loud. She moved a little closer on the couch. Perry didn't shift away. The space between them was no longer guarded.

"You handled tonight better than anyone else could have," Tess said. "And you're still standing. That says something."

Perry met her eyes. "You were there the whole time. I couldn't have done any of it alone."

Tess let out a breath. "We're a good team."

"We are," Perry said quietly.

The room went still in a way that felt different from the quiet before. Not tension. Not shock. Just an awareness of where they were and what they had just gone through together, the kind of night that rearranged people whether they planned for it or not.

Tess reached out and touched his arm. Simple. Direct. Perry didn't flinch. He covered her hand with his.

She leaned in first. A small shift of her weight. A check-in he could have ignored. He didn't. He met her halfway, and they kissed with the kind of certainty that didn't need discussion.

There was nothing rushed about it. No desperation. Just two people who had crossed a line without trying to and didn't want to step back.

When the kiss broke Tess rested her forehead against his. "You're sure," she asked.

"Yes," Perry said. No hesitation.

Tess kissed him again, deeper this time, then stood and took his hand. Perry followed her toward the bedroom. Neither of them said anything. Neither of them needed to.

Otis lifted his head, watched them go, then relaxed again, calm and unbothered.

The door closed softly.

The apartment stayed quiet for the rest of the night.

Chapter Thirteen – As If

Morning came in quietly. Perry woke first and stayed still for a moment, getting used to the shape of the room and the warmth beside him. Tess slept on her stomach, one arm over the pillow, her hair a little messy. She looked peaceful, something he hadn't seen last night.

Otis lay on the floor near the door, awake and watching. The second Perry shifted, Otis's tail moved once, slow and steady, like a greeting.

Perry eased out of bed without waking Tess. He poured water, checked the street from the window, and listened for anything out of place. Nothing unusual. Just a normal morning in a neighborhood that didn't know how strange the night before had been.

Tess stepped into the doorway a minute later, wearing one of his shirts. She didn't look embarrassed or unsure. Just present.

"Morning," she said.

"Morning."

She walked over and kissed him once, soft and certain, then looked at the window. "Any sign of him?"

"No."

"We still stay careful," Tess said. "He didn't give up just because he lost us last night."

"I know."

Otis came over and nudged Tess's leg. She rubbed his head. "We're keeping you safe," she said. "All three of us."

Perry watched them and felt that same quiet shift from last night settle in a little deeper.

Tess turned back to him. "You have a self-tape to do."

"Yeah," he said. "I'll knock it out in an hour."

"And you should call your mom."

He gave a tired smile. "She'll want the whole update."

"Give her the version she can handle," Tess said. "The rest stays here."

Perry nodded. "What about you?"

"I'm starting the search," Tess said. "Ownership laws, lost-and-found rules, anything that helps us keep Otis permanently. I'll make a list and we'll work through it today."

"You don't have to do all that."

She stepped closer, close enough that he could feel her breath. "I know I don't. I'm doing it because I'm in this with you."

Perry kissed her, just once, and she rested her hand against his chest before pulling back.

"We'll figure it out," she said.

"We will."

Otis watched them with a steady calm that made him look almost confident in the outcome.

Perry grabbed his phone and opened his mother's voicemail. Tess moved to the table with her laptop. The apartment felt different now. Not less dangerous. But more solid. Like they had shifted from surviving to planning.

And for the first time since the head injury, Perry knew he wasn't alone with any of it.

Chapter Fourteen – Noticed

Tess looked up from her laptop when Perry put on his jacket.

"You're heading out?," she said.

"I need to check something," Perry replied. "Keep looking up legal options for making Otis ours. Anything about ownership transfers, abandonment, whatever applies."

Tess watched him carefully. "You're going to his house?"

"Yes."

"Take your phone. And be careful."

"I will," he said. "I'm not going near the door. I just want information."

He left without Otis. Bringing the dog to that house again wasn't an option. The walk was quick and quiet. Perry didn't rush. He didn't look around like someone casing a place. He looked like a man out for a morning errand.

When he crossed the street, everything appeared normal. A neighbor sweeping leaves. Someone unloading groceries. A kid pushing a bike with a flat tire. The house itself looked unremarkable, the same as it did the night they took Otis.

Perry approached the mailbox near the curb. He stopped as if checking his phone for something, though he already knew what he wanted.

NATHAN.
Daniel Nathan.

He repeated the name once in his head.

A faint sound drew his attention back to the house. Not loud. Not sharp. Just a quick muffled impact from inside. The kind of sound normal walls were supposed to hide. No one else turned. A man jogging past didn't even break stride.

Perry shifted a few steps down the sidewalk and angled his head slightly, isolating what he needed to hear without showing it.

Another sound followed.
A woman's voice. Quiet. Strained. He couldn't hear the words.
Then the man's voice, low and hostile, carrying a tone he recognized instantly.

A scuffle. A hit.

The woman cried out, muted but clear enough for Perry to catch. Not clear enough for anyone else; the street kept moving as if nothing had happened.

He focused more tightly, filtering out car engines and footsteps until only the house remained.

Then the smell reached him.

Blood.

Not a lot, but enough to know there was real harm happening behind that door.

Perry didn't move. He kept his posture relaxed, phone in hand, like he was checking a message. Inside, the house was chaos. Outside, the world stayed exactly the same.

He stepped behind a parked car, giving himself a little cover while he listened long enough to confirm what he already knew: the woman was hurt, and the man was hurting her.

He typed a message to Tess:

Found his name.
Heading back now.

He didn't add anything else. This wasn't the kind of thing to explain over text.

He walked away from the house with the same controlled pace he used approaching it. Not fast. Not slow. Nothing to attract attention. Just a man finishing a walk on a quiet street.

As he turned into his apartment building, one thing was certain:

Something was very wrong in Daniel Nathan's house. And Perry and Tess were the only ones who knew enough to do something about it.

***

Tess opened the door before Perry knocked. He had heard her pacing from halfway down the hallway. Her steps were tight, stopping and starting, tension rolling off her long before she appeared. Not fear. Just pressure with nowhere to go.

Otis stood beside her, watching Perry with steady focus.

"What happened?," Tess asked, voice low.

"His name is Daniel Nathan," Perry said. He stepped inside and locked the door behind him.

Tess waited. She could tell there was more.

Perry exhaled. "There's a woman in the house. He hit her. More than once."

Tess's expression tightened, her focus narrowing instantly.

"She's hurt," Perry added quietly.

"And no one else heard?," Tess asked.

"No," Perry replied. "Only me."

Otis moved closer and planted near Tess's feet.

Perry leaned against the counter. "I didn't call the police. They wouldn't believe me. How could I explain it. If I told them the truth, they'd think I was crazy."

Tess didn't argue. "Yeah, but we have to help her. We can't just sit here. What are we going to do?"

Perry stepped away from the counter and sat at the table. Tess closed her laptop, then opened it again, grounding herself.

"We're dealing with something real," she said quietly. "If he keeps hurting her, the next time could be worse."

Perry nodded once. "I know."

"And if we show up or confront him, we could make things worse for her," Tess said. "He'll hide her or shut everything down. We can't do that."

"We won't," Perry said.

Tess pulled her laptop closer. "I'm going to look into him. Public records. Anything that gives us an opening."

Perry watched her, steady and focused. "Stay on him. I'll stay alert for anything we can use."

Tess nodded. "Good. That keeps us moving."

Perry breathed out slowly. "We'll get her help, Tess."

"Yes," she said. "We will."

Otis lifted his head at their voices, then dropped it again, calm.

Tess stood, moved to him, and kissed him once, steady and sure. "Film your tape," she said softly. "I'll keep working. We'll talk later."

Perry returned the kiss, then went to set up in the other   room.
Tess pulled her chair closer to the table and began typing fast, focused.

The apartment felt different now.
Not lighter.
More aligned.

They weren't reacting anymore.
They were stepping into something together.

Chapter Fifteen – Close

Morning arrived into the apartment without much conversation. Not because anything was wrong between them, but because both were already thinking ahead. Perry took Otis out the back way. Tess watched from the window until they came back inside.

She grabbed her bag. "I'll see what I can find at work. I have better access to public records, civil filings, anything that's legitimately accessible there."

Perry nodded. "I'll stay alert. He's still out there looking."

They left together and split at the corner.

Perry walked to the café with his hood low. He moved through the morning rush smoothly, doing the tasks he could do even half-distracted. Every time the door opened, his attention flicked toward it. Not nervous. Watchful. He knew Daniel was still out there searching, and Perry didn't want to cross paths with him again without knowing it first.

He noticed flyers shifting on the community board. Someone had moved the missing dog flyer higher. Someone else had taken a phone number from the tear-off tabs. Small details, but they stuck with him.

Meanwhile, at the law office, Tess used her break the way a paralegal actually could.

Daniel Nathan.
She checked civil dockets.
Lease disputes.
Noise complaints tied to old addresses.
Property ownership records.
Prior filings from neighbors.
Nothing criminal.
Nothing actionable.
But enough instability to confirm what Perry had already sensed.

She texted him.

Tess: Found civil issues. Nothing major, but he's got a pattern.
Perry: He's still looking.
Tess: For Otis?
Perry: Yeah.

She tucked her phone back into her bag and returned to drafting motions, her attention split but steady.

Perry walked home after his shift, taking a quieter route. He didn't see Daniel. He didn't hear anything unusual. But he stayed alert the whole way.

Tess arrived at the apartment a few minutes later.

When the door shut behind her, the day finally seemed to settle.

Tess opened her laptop. "I can't trigger anything from my office. Not legally. But if someone reports something believable---yelling, threats, something happening outside---police can do a welfare check."

Perry sat across from her. "So we wait for something public. Something anyone could notice."

Tess nodded. "Daniel is volatile. He won't keep everything behind closed doors forever."

"And when it slips," Perry said, "we report it."

"Anonymous," Tess added. "Specific enough to be taken seriously."

Perry leaned forward slightly. "We'll help her."

"Yes," Tess said. "We will."

Otis lay down between them, quiet and watchful.

The conversation subsided, not with answers, but with the simple relief of saying things out loud. They let the room stay quiet for a while, neither of them rushing to fill it.

***

The café was already half-full when Perry stepped inside. The bell over the door chimed, steady and familiar. Something in the air felt wrong. A scent put him on alert. A rhythm in the room that pulled at him.

He pensively tied his apron and moved toward the pastry case, then he saw it, the flyer taped to the espresso machine.

Not the first one he had seen.

A new one.

Same blurry photo. Same cheap printer ink.

But the headline had changed.

STOLEN DOG
Reward. No questions asked.

The earlier flyer, the one someone had tacked to the community board days ago, had said Lost Dog.
That one had read like a plea.
This one read like a charge.

Rina came out from the back carrying a sleeve of lids. She followed his stare and stopped.

"Yeah. That showed up first thing this morning."

Perry peeled it off the machine. The tape resisted more than he expected, and the paper bent at the corner.

"It's different," Perry said quietly.

"From 'lost' to 'stolen,'" Rina said. "That is not a small step."

Perry folded the flyer once. "That terrib---."

She looked at him directly. "Perry, is this Otis?"

He didn't dodge it. "Yeah."

"And the guy is calling you a thief."

"He doesn't know who has him," Perry said. "He is just trying to ramp it up."

Rina watched him closely, reading his face the way she read customers when they were about to complain. "Then why put the flyer here?"

"He is putting them up everywhere."

She studied him for a moment. "Alright. What is going on?"

Perry set the folded flyer on the counter. "Otis was not stolen. He was neglected. Badly. The first time I saw him he was shaking so hard he could barely stand. His leg was infected. He was alone in a yard with no food or water."

Rina's jaw tightened. Not shock. Just anger aimed in the right direction.

"And the man?," she asked. "What's his deal?"

"Not someone a dog should go back to," Perry said. "That is all I can say."

Rina let out a slow breath. "Then this flyer is trash?"

"Yeah."

"You are not giving Otis back?"

"No."

"Good."

She crossed her arms and leaned against the counter. "If this spills into the café, I want to know. I

90

can handle rude customers, but I do not want some guy storming in here with accusations."

"It will not happen," Perry said. "Not here."

"That is less comforting than you think."

"I am handling it."

She nodded once. "Alright. If anyone asks, I know nothing. And if this guy walks in here, I will keep him talking until you are out the back."

"You do not have to---"

"I am doing it for the dog," she said with a wry smile. "Not you. And Perry, you don't need to lie to me"

A small breath broke out of him. Not relief exactly, but something close.

"I'm sorry"

The morning rush rose and fell. Perry worked without glancing at every person who walked through the door. He still listened. He still stayed aware. But he did not brace the way he had yesterday.

When his shift ended, he grabbed his jacket. Rina was wiping the front counter.

"Text if anything changes," she said.

"I will."

"Perry."

He paused.

"Be careful."

He nodded once and headed outside.

The air felt sharp on his face. The folded flyer stayed in his pocket, heavier than paper should be.

The first flyer had said Lost Dog.
This one said Stolen Dog.

Daniel was not just searching anymore.

He was pushing.

***

Tess came in quietly, nudging the door shut with her hip while she carried her coat and a few office folders. Otis trotted over immediately, tail low but steady. She set the folders on the table and crouched to rub the side of his face before taking off her coat.

"You look tired," Perry said.

"Long day," she said. "Yours?"

He pulled the folded flyer from his jacket pocket and handed it to her. Tess opened it. Her expression changed as soon as she read the headline.

"Stolen Dog," she said. "He's getting serious now."

"Rina found it taped to the front door when she opened," Perry said. "She put it on the machine so I would see it."

Tess looked over the smaller text, the phrasing sharper than the earlier flyer. She set it on the table, jaw tense.

"He wants whoever has him to look like a criminal," she said.

"He wants someone caught," Perry said. "And if he finds us first, I don't think he stops at calling the cops."

Tess opened one of the folders she had brought home. "I talked to someone today. A friend I went to school with who works admin at the precinct. She can't give me anything formal, but she gave me background."

Perry sat. Otis leaned against his leg.

"Daniel Nathan has a record," Tess said. "Not big things. Petty theft. Disorderly conduct. Fights. Trespassing. Harassment. Fines. He slips through every time."

"So he knows how to push limits," Perry said.

"Yes. And he has no active warrants, so no one is watching him," Tess said. "My friend said he gets out of control. Loud fights. Things breaking. Neighbors calling because they are scared."

Perry looked toward the window, though the blinds were closed. "He is getting closer. People have seen me with Otis. That kind of gossip spreads fast, word gets around."

"It probably reached him already," Tess said. "He doesn't know you or your building, but he knows the neighborhood."

Perry rubbed the side of his neck. "We cannot wait for him to get lucky."

Tess nodded. "I agree. The more attention he stirs up, the easier it is for him to point fingers. And once he does that, clearing our names gets harder."

"Why is he so bent on getting Otis back? He practically abandoned him in his own yard."

"I'm not so sure this is about Otis anymore." Tess replied.

The room hushed into a steady quiet.

"He is not backing off," Tess said. "He wants this to land on somebody."

"Then we move first," Perry said. "Make it harder for him to act without someone noticing."

"And easier to get help for the woman if he slips," Tess said. "We just need one opening."

Otis let out a low sound.

Alert.

Perry reached down and smoothed his fur. "He feels it."

"So do we," Tess said. "But we are not letting Daniel control us."

They sat for a moment, the direction finally clear.

"We will help that woman," Tess said. "And we will keep him safe." She nodded at Otis.

Perry looked at the flyer one more time, then set it aside. "He is not stopping. He is going to keep coming."

"Yes," Tess said. "Which means we cannot sit still anymore."

She closed her folder.

Otis lifted his head, watching them both.

They were not waiting for Daniel to make the next move.

They were planning theirs.

Chapter Sixteen – Move

Perry left just after the streetlights flicked on. He locked the door behind him and started walking, keeping to the quieter streets out of habit more than caution. The air had cooled enough that every smell sat lower to the ground. Concrete. Old garbage from a loose bin. Hot metal fading from parked cars. Nothing sharp enough to matter.

He reached Daniel's house after a short, steady walk. Before stepping closer, he stopped and let the neighborhood settle around him. Smells drifted from open windows and worn porch wood. One scent stood out: Daniel's. Cigarettes, cheap soap, and a sour edge that stuck to the back of the throat.

He moved closer.

Daniel's house looked exactly as before: a porch that needed sweeping, a crooked screen door, an upstairs light casting a dim glow across the siding. Perry stayed across the street at first, pacing slowly like anyone killing time on their phone. But he wasn't killing time. He was listening.

There. Footsteps. Heavy, uneven, pacing without rhythm. Something fell. A muttered curse. Then the footsteps headed toward the door.

Perry shifted his weight just slightly and kept his head down.

The door opened. Daniel stepped out, locked it with one irritated twist, and gave the street a quick, unfocused scan. He walked toward the corner, his stride rushed and frustrated. Perry tracked the sound until Daniel's footsteps faded into the general noise of the block and his scent thinned as he moved farther away.

Only then did Perry cross the street.

He didn't go to the porch. He suspected she wouldn't open the door, and he didn't want to force her into refusing. Instead he moved along the narrow strip at the side of the house, staying on the dirt where his steps stayed soft.

Halfway down, he stopped. Listened.

Someone was inside. Not moving around. Just breathing. Slow. Measured. A person who knew how to stay quiet.

Perry stepped closer and tapped the side window with one knuckle. Not loud. Not timid. Just enough.

Silence.
Then the curtain shifted.

A woman's face appeared in the narrow gap. Early thirties. Exhausted eyes. She stiffened.

Perry kept his voice low. "I'm not here to bother you. I just want to know if you're alright."

Her voice was barely a whisper through the glass. "Who are you?"

"Someone who knows about the dog," he said. "That's all."

Her expression changed, not recognition, but understanding. Someone involved. Someone she shouldn't be talking to.

"You can't be here," she whispered. "If he comes back---"

"I won't stay long," Perry said. "I promise."

She looked toward the front of the house, weighing risk against time. "Please. Go."

"I will," Perry said. "I just need to know if you're safe."

She let out a small, empty breath. "Safe isn't something that happens here."

"Do you want help?" he asked.

"No," she said quickly. "I can't. Not now."

"I'm not asking you to leave," Perry said. "Just---if you ever need someone to call, I can be that person."

She hesitated. Then: "You have the dog?"

"Yes."

A flicker of relief crossed her face before fear pulled it back down. "He wasn't good to him," she whispered. "You know that?"

"I saw enough."

She pressed her palm lightly to the glass, not reaching for him, just bracing herself. "Please don't tell him you came here. He'll blame me."

"I won't say anything," Perry said. "And I'll be gone before he gets close."

She nodded once. A survival nod, not trust.

Perry stepped back. The curtain dropped fast.

He retraced his steps along the side of the house, listening for anything that didn't fit. No new footsteps. No shift in scent on the air. No sign Daniel had doubled back.

Only when he reached the sidewalk did he let his shoulders ease.

She was alive. She was afraid.
And Daniel wasn't done.

***

Tess buzzed him in fast, like she hadn't stepped far from the intercom. When she opened her apartment door and saw his face, she didn't ask anything. She just reached for him, her hand closing around the front of his jacket, pulling him inside before the hallway air could settle.

Perry stepped in, and she shut the door behind them. The city noise dulled. What was left was her and him, close enough that she could see the tension in his shoulders.

"You talked to her," Tess said softly.

"Yes."

The answer lingered in the air. Tess moved closer, her hand sliding along his shoulder.

"Come here."

He did. She pressed her forehead briefly to his chest, grounding herself in the shape of him. He rested a hand at her waist, steadying both of them without needing to think about it.

They stayed like that until the silence set. Then he told her what happened at the window---the whispering, the fear, the way the woman watched the street even while speaking to him. Tess didn't interrupt. She kept a hand on him the entire time, brushing lightly across his arm in small, instinctive movements.

When he finished, she exhaled quietly and lifted her head to meet his eyes.

"Alright."

She wasn't surprised. She wasn't shaken. She was absorbing it.

Tess eased back just enough to look at him fully. "You can't stay at your place anymore. Daniel's house is too close to your apartment. It's too easy for him to notice something."

"I know," Perry said.

"Then stay here," she told him. "You and Otis. For now."

No hesitation. No awkwardness. Just truth said out loud.

Perry nodded once. "Okay."

Something eased in her posture, the kind of release that comes when a decision lands exactly where it should. She guided him to the couch and sat close enough that their legs touched.

"Tell me what you're thinking," she said.

"Track him," Perry said. "Follow him properly. Most people are creatures of habit. They go to the same places, talk to the same people, repeat themselves without realizing it. Daniel won't be any different. If I watch long enough, I'll see where he leaves openings."

Tess nodded, her hand sliding along his forearm until her fingers found his. "And once he gives us that opening?"

"We use it," Perry said. "Something public. Something he can't hide inside the apartment."

"That fits," Tess said. "If he threatens someone on the street, breaks something that isn't his, gets loud enough that neighbors notice, those things get response. And if he's carrying anything he shouldn't, even better."

"He'll give us something," Perry said.

Her voice softened. "Just come here after. That's all I need."

"I will."

She leaned in and kissed him---slow, warm, steady. The kind of kiss that wasn't about urgency but about the realization of how close they were becoming. When they parted, she rested her forehead against his.

"You're here now," she whispered.

"So are you," he said.

The room slowed around them, full but quiet, just two people who stopped holding distance they never wanted in the first place.

Tess tucked herself against his side, her hand resting over his. "We'll work from here," she said.

"We will," Perry answered.

Outside, the city kept moving.

Inside, their next step was already set---together.

Chapter Seventeen – Damage

Perry was half a block from the café when the air shifted. Not a change in temperature. A scent. Sharp, close, unmistakable.

Daniel.

It hung low across the sidewalk, caught in the damp of the morning and the stale exhaust drifting between buildings. Perry slowed, letting the noise of the street fall into the background.

Daniel was nearby.

He approached the café carefully, steps quiet, listening for footfalls that didn't match the rhythm of the early crowd. Then he saw him.

Daniel came out of the front door of the shop, jaw tight, shoulders wound, scanning the street. His agitation carried in every movement.

Perry stepped back into the recessed entry of a closed boutique. Daniel walked right past him, the tension rolling off him in a way that no one else on the street seemed to register.

Only when Daniel turned the corner did Perry move again. He circled through the alley and slipped into the rear entrance of the café.

Rina stood waiting for him, arms folded, eyes uneasy. "Perry---"

He knew that tone.

"He was just here," she said. "A guy named Daniel. Said he heard someone saw his dog with a man who worked at the shop and described you."

Perry stayed still.

"I told him I couldn't give out personal info. Said I didn't know anything." She glanced toward the front windows. "I don't think he believed me."

Perry offered a small nod of gratitude.

Rina exhaled sharply and rubbed her palms down the sides of her apron. "I can't keep you on. Not with him walking in here. If the police get pulled into this, the shop could get dragged into it too. I'm sorry."

"I understand," Perry said.

"I'm really sorry," she repeated, and this time she stepped forward and hugged him. Quick, firm, sincere. "You're a good guy, Perry. But this is---too much."

He didn't argue. When she let go, he slipped out the rear door, hood low, posture relaxed enough to avoid drawing attention but aware of every sound around him.

He walked two blocks, listening. Daniel's scent drifted faintly through the morning air, pulled east by the slow churn of traffic and shifting pockets of wind.

Perry followed.

He didn't rush. He didn't stalk. He simply kept Daniel in range, across streets, behind parked cars, within crowds that masked him without effort. His senses drew a rough map of Daniel's movement: where his footsteps dragged, where his breath quickened, where his focus kept darting to porches, alleys, doorways.

Daniel was searching. Not wandering. Searching with purpose.

And Perry had nothing but time now.

Daniel moved through several blocks, cutting across intersections too quickly, asking questions Perry couldn't hear word-for-word but didn't need to. His pace was wrong---too eager, too tight. A man chasing something he thought he could almost grab.

Perry stayed opposite him, just out of sight lines, keeping the rhythm of Daniel's movements centered in his awareness.

By late morning, Daniel finally headed toward his house. He walked up the porch steps, unlocked the door with a frustrated twist of his shoulder, and disappeared inside.

Perry stopped beneath the canopy of a street tree across the road. Its branches offered partial cover, enough for him to watch the entrance without being watched.

Daniel was closer than ever.
And he was closing in fast on the truth.

What Daniel didn't know, what he couldn't imagine, was that Perry was closing in too.

Their circles were tightening at the same pace.
One out of anger.
One out of resolve.

The afternoon air fell still around the block, heavy with tension neither man could see.

And from where he stood, Perry waited.

***

Daniel left the house late in the afternoon, moving with the same steady pace Perry had seen before. Perry followed at a distance, letting the street carry him along while he watched the patterns reveal themselves.

Daniel made brief stops along the way. Quiet exchanges. People appearing from doorways and alleys, then disappearing again. Nothing loud, nothing careless. He checked corners before turning, glanced at reflective glass without slowing, moved like someone who knew exactly where attention lived and how to avoid it.

By the time Daniel returned home, the rhythm was clear.

Perry waited across the street until the block settled, then turned toward Tess's apartment.

His time spent following Daniel was paying off. He was getting to know his rhythm.

Tomorrow he'd try to follow again, if Daniel went anywhere at all.

Chapter Eighteen – No Cover

The morning was quiet when Perry woke in Tess's apartment. Tess was warm against him, one arm resting across his chest. At the foot of the bed, Otis was curled in a tight circle, head lifting the moment Perry shifted.

Perry slipped out from under Tess's arm and reached for his phone. Otis stretched, hopped down, and followed him into the living room.

A new email waited at the top of his inbox.

His agent.

He opened it.

Call-back. In person. Supporting lead.

A real audition, not another self-tape. Perry let the words settle without chasing them. Otis pressed his head lightly against Perry's shin, sensing the small change in his breath.

Tess stirred in the bedroom. "You okay?" she murmured.

"Yeah. Just checking email."

She reached toward him sleepily. "Come back."

He did, briefly. Otis hopped up beside Tess, occupying the warm spot Perry left.

When Tess finally got up and left for work, Perry clipped a leash to Otis's collar and walked the neighborhood. He passed two cafés, a bakery with an espresso bar, and a corner shop with a handwritten "Help Wanted" sign. Otis sniffed every tree they passed, unaware of the new job Perry was quietly considering.

Back near the subway entrance, Perry stopped at an electronics stand and bought a camera the size of a button. He held it beside his glasses. Barely noticeable. He tested the angle in a storefront window. It would work.

Back at Tess's apartment, Otis sat by the window while Perry set the camera on the kitchen table and waited for her.

She came home just after six, cheeks flushed from the cold. Otis trotted over and pressed against her legs. She scratched behind his ears, then caught sight of the small camera.

"What's that?"

"For tomorrow," Perry said. "If he leaves the house, I can actually record something."

Tess nodded, taking off her coat. "Did he go out today?"

"No," Perry said. "Or if he did, I missed it."

Otis circled twice and lay down between them.

Tess filled two glasses with water and handed one to Perry. "Tell me the rest."

He told her about the morning. About the call-back. About the cafés near her place. About the quiet block around Daniel's house. Otis lifted his head occasionally, tracking Perry's voice.

"Would you take the part?" Tess asked.

"If everything lines up," Perry said. "But I'm not stepping away from this."

She nodded. "Then we see where the timing lands."

His phone buzzed.

Rina.

He answered. "Hey."

Her voice was strained. "He came back."

Perry didn't speak.

"That man. The one looking for the dog." A breath. "He walked in again today. Looked around the whole shop."

Otis's head lifted, ears pointed toward the phone.

"I told him I hadn't seen anyone who matched what he described. He kept pushing, asking if anyone ever brought a black dog in. I said no."

Perry let her speak.

"I'm not doing that again," she said. "I wanted you to know. That's it."

"You did fine," Perry said.

"I hope so." She hung up.

Tess was watching him. Otis padded over and rested his chin on Perry's knee.

"He's closing in," she said.

"Yeah."

She stepped closer and rested her hand along his jaw, brushing lightly over his skin. "Come home safe tomorrow. That's all I want."

"I will."

She kissed him once, soft and certain. Otis circled their legs, then stopped at their feet with a sigh like the house finally felt full again.

Later, they ate. Talked. Let the evening wind down. Otis followed them into the bedroom and climbed onto the bed as if he'd lived there for years.

Perry placed the small camera beside his glasses on the nightstand. Tess curled against him, her arm across his ribs. Otis lay pressed against Perry's leg, warm and breathing steadily.

Perry stayed awake a moment, listening to both of them, thinking about Daniel's door, the call-back, the street he'd walked yesterday.

Tomorrow he'd try to follow again.

He closed his eyes. Tess breathed softly. Otis shifted closer.

***

Daniel woke earlier than usual. The room was dim, colder than he liked, and the house was silent. No bacon. No coffee. No noise from the kitchen. The quiet irritated him.

He pushed himself out of bed and walked down the hall. The house carried its usual stale mix of old smoke, grease that clung to everything, and last night's whiskey evaporating off the counter. He moved through it with the impatience of someone who expected the morning to be shaped around him before he arrived in it.

She was in the kitchen, but not where she should've been. Rinsing a mug instead of at the stove. Still in her T-shirt. Still slow. She startled when he came in.

"No breakfast?" he said.

"I---I thought you were still asleep," she said, rushing toward the stove. "I'm making it now."

"Yeah." He let the word flatten into irritation. "I don't have time to stand around."

She cracked the eggs too fast, bits of shell falling into the bowl. She tried to hide it with her hand. Luckily, Daniel didn't notice. His eyes had landed on the empty place where the dog bowl used to be. The space annoyed him, not because the dog was gone, but because the whole situation reminded him he'd been made a fool of.

"That couple," he said, pulling a fork from the drawer with more force than needed. "Walking around like they can take something of mine and feel good about it."

She didn't respond. She never did. It wasn't a conversation.

Daniel sat at the table, tapping the fork against his plate even though there was nothing on it yet. She got the pan hot, her movements tight and practiced, rushing without looking frantic.

"You knew what time I had to leave," he said, not acknowledging that he'd woken nearly an hour before he ever did.

She plated the food and set it in front of him. Daniel ate quickly, aggressively, shoveling in the eggs with short, sharp motions. He wasn't tasting anything. His mind was already out the door.

"They think they can pull something like that," he said, dropping the fork onto the plate with a hard clatter. "I'll handle them."

He didn't look at her when he left. The door slammed hard enough to make the stove rattle.

Outside, Perry stood in the narrow strip of shadow between two rowhouses. The cold air carried Daniel's scent as distinctly as a fingerprint: stale smoke, alcohol, a hot, sweaty mist of anger that had once soaked into Otis's fur.

Daniel came off the porch with a determined stride, muttering to himself, jaw tight, already building the story of how he'd make someone pay for stealing from him.

Perry waited until the footsteps eased into their steady rhythm before stepping out from the shadows, breath controlled, attention open, tracking the danger moving down the block.

***

Tess was halfway through sorting a stack of case summaries when her phone buzzed on the corner of her desk. She glanced at the display, saw the name, and answered before the second ring.

"Hey," her friend said, voice low in the way people used when they didn't want anyone else catching pieces of the conversation. "I need to own up to something. I missed a detail earlier when I ran your guy."

Tess straightened in her chair. "What detail?"

"He doesn't have warrants, that part's true. But he's on parole. Drug possession with an illegal handgun." A calm exhale. "It was sitting right in front of me. I don't know how I missed it."

Tess let the information land. The dull fluorescent lights hummed above her. The office clatter faded under the weight of what she was hearing.

"How long left on his parole?" she asked.

"Few months. If he screws up, even a little, they'll pull him in fast. And with his history, it won't take much."

Tess closed her eyes for a moment, not out of fear, but something closer to relief, an opening, however narrow, that hadn't existed before. "Thanks," she said quietly. "Really."

"I'll send you the details," her friend said. "Just---be careful. A guy like that, who knows?"

"I know," Tess said.

She hung up and stared at her computer screen, the text blurring for a second. It wasn't a solution, not yet, but it was something she could hold onto, something they could use.

After work, she picked up carryout, Thai from the place Perry liked, and headed home. The apartment smelled strongly of dog shampoo and wet towels, a combination she wouldn't have expected a few months ago.

Perry was already back, Otis stretched across the rug, still a little wet from a bath he must have just received. Perry looked up when she entered, the uncertainty he'd carried earlier replaced with something steadier.

"How was it?" she asked, setting the food on the counter.

"Uneventful," he said, washing his hands. "He stuck to his usual places. The camera worked, though. Clean footage."

She nodded. "Good. That's good."

They unpacked dinner, the quiet of the apartment softer than the quiet in Daniel's kitchen that morning. Otis nudged his head against Tess's knee, waiting for a piece of chicken she pretended not to notice him begging for.

"There's something else," she said finally.

Perry looked over.

"I got a call from my friend at the precinct. She had missed something in Daniel's file. He's on parole. Drug charge with a gun." She watched Perry's expression tighten, not with fear but with understanding.

"Well, that's actually great!" he said excitedly, "how long?"

"A few months. If he does anything wrong---anything---they can take him in. We don't have to depend on luck. We might actually have leverage."

Perry leaned back slightly, the weight in the room shifting. Not lifting, exactly. But redistributing. "That's something we can work with," he said.

Otis settled between them, head on his paws, unaware of the way the world outside was slowly rearranging itself.

They ate together, the conversation quiet but hopeful. It wasn't over, not even close. But for the first time, they weren't just reacting. They had a real chance. And Daniel Nathan, for all his bluster, had just become vulnerable in a way he probably didn't even realize.

Chapter Nineteen – Contact

Perry had already taken the mirror off the wall and wrapped it in a blanket. The dresser was the last thing left in the apartment. It sat in the center of the room with the drawers taped shut, the corners worn from years of use. He didn't linger on it. The apartment sounded different without furniture, his footsteps sharper, the room giving everything back to him. He slid his phone into his pocket and waited.

The buyer pulled up in a gray SUV and parked partly on the curb. The engine idled unevenly. Perry heard it before he saw the vehicle. When the man got out, Perry caught the smell of stale air and cologne that pushed ahead of him. Middle-aged, clean jacket, polite smile. His voice matched it.

They lifted the dresser together, one end at a time. Perry adjusted his grip when the weight shifted. He felt the strain in his forearms and the pressure in his ears from the room going quiet behind him. At the doorway, the dresser scraped lightly against the trim. The sound stuck with him longer than it should have.

Outside, they eased it into the back of the SUV. The buyer pulled straps from the cargo area. The nylon hissed as he tightened them. Perry stepped back and scanned the street without thinking about it. Nothing out of place. No sudden movement.

A little way down the block, in front of his house, Daniel Nathan sat in his car with the engine off and windows up. His phone in hand as he scrolled through his messages. He happened to look and recognize Perry.

Perry closed the building door and stood on the sidewalk longer than necessary. The street noise felt uneven, a gap where something should have been steady. He crossed to the row of mail slots beside the entrance and opened his. He took the mail, folded it once, and tucked it under his arm.

He walked down the street and around the corner, disappearing form sight.

Daniel watched until Perry was gone.

He stayed in his car until the sidewalk emptied, then crossed the street at an unhurried pace. He stopped in front of the mail slots and looked at them without touching anything. The labels were small but readable. He focused on the one Perry had opened.

Perry Heller.

Daniel stepped back. The name memorized. A face now had something attached to it.

He returned to his car and sat behind the wheel with the engine still off.

He was getting closer.

***

Perry was at Tess's apartment when his phone rang. Late morning. The place was quiet in a way that felt earned, not empty. Otis lay near the window, head up, watching the street below.

Rina's name lit the screen.

Perry answered before the second ring.

"I'm at the shop," she said.

The background came through immediately. Refrigeration units cycling. Traffic filtered through glass. Her voice was steady, but there was strain in it now.

"Okay," Perry said.

"I opened about twenty minutes ago," she said. "There was something taped to the front door."

His attention narrowed.

"I took it down right away," she said.

A brief pause.

"It's another one," she said. "Same setup as before."

Perry closed his eyes.

"It says FOUND," she said. "Your name's underneath."

The room went still. Perry noticed the faint tick of the wall clock, the low whirr of the ceiling fan. Otis shifted near the window but stayed where he was.

"How long was it there?," Perry asked.

"I don't know," Rina said. "Not long. Long enough."

"Anyone else around?"

"I can't guarantee no one saw it."

He let that sit.

"There wasn't anything else on it," she said. "No number. No message."

Perry didn't try to imagine how Daniel had gotten his name. There were too many possibilities, and none of them mattered yet.

"I wanted you to hear it from me," Rina said. "Not later. Not from someone else."

"I'm glad you called," Perry said.

She exhaled, a controlled breath that didn't quite settle.

"I'm not mad at you," she said. "And I'm not backing away. I just need you to understand that this scared me. This is getting really fucking creepy."

"I know," Perry said.

"I opened the door and it was right there," she continued. "On the glass. Where anyone could see it. I don't know how long it had been up. I don't know who walked by before me." She said, repeating herself.

"Ok."

"I'll cover for you if I need to," she said. "I just---I don't want to be surprised by this anymore."

"You shouldn't be," Perry said.

"For what it's worth," she added, quieter now, "this feels closer than before."

"I agree."

They stayed on the line a moment longer, the café's low hum filling the space between them.

"Be careful," Rina said.

"I will," Perry replied.

The call ended.

Perry lowered the phone. Tess was watching him from across the room.

"Another flyer," she said, overhearing the conversation.

"Yes."

He didn't speak right away. He listened to the apartment, the ordinary sounds suddenly more exposed.

"It had my name on it," he said.

Tess absorbed that.

"So he knows who you are," she said.

"Yes."

"And you don't know how?"

"No."

Tess nodded once. "That changes things."

Perry didn't argue.

Otis remained near the window, alert, tracking movement outside.

Perry finally said, "We can't wait this out."

Tess met his eyes. "I know."

Nothing else needed to be said. The situation had shifted again, not louder, but tighter.

Chapter Twenty – After The Noise

Perry was standing at the counter when his phone buzzed. Not a call. A message.

He almost ignored it. The apartment had fallen into a tense quiet that made interruptions feel intrusive. Otis lay near the window. Tess sat at the table, laptop open, not really looking at it.

The screen lit again.

His agent's name.

Perry unlocked the phone.

Got it.
You're in.
They want you in Toronto.
Two weeks.
Eight weeks total.
Pays well. Call me.

Perry read it once. Then again. Slower.

Tess noticed the change immediately. His breathing shifted. Not faster. Thinner.

"You got it," she said.

"Yes."

Her posture changed. Not excitement. Attention.

"When?"

"Two weeks," Perry said. "Canada. Two months."

She closed the laptop.

"That's the window?," she said.

"Yeah."

Silence stretched between them.

"He knows your name now," Tess said.

"Yeah."

"And if you leave," she said, "this doesn't pause."

"No," Perry said.

Otis moved away from the window and sat, alert, watching them.

"This is the break," Perry said. Not as a pitch. As a fact. "It's momentum."

"I know," Tess said.

"And if I take it," he said, "I'm leaving you here with him still after us."

She didn't look away. "Would you do that?"

"I won't."

She was relieved, although she knew the answer.

"So we don't wait," Tess said.

Perry felt the shift. Decision replacing tension.

"He's on parole," Perry said. "He's already pushing it."

"Then we stop letting him do it quietly," Tess said.

Otis stayed where he was, ears angled toward them.

"We need something decisive," Perry said. "Not pressure. Not warnings."

"And fast," Tess said.

Perry glanced at the clock. The sound felt sharper now.

"Two weeks," he said.

Tess nodded. "Then that's the timeline."

Perry picked up his phone and typed.

Got it.
I'll call you soon.

He didn't send it yet.

This wasn't about work versus safety. It was about whether he could step away without leaving her exposed.

He set the phone down.

They both knew what came next wouldn't be careful. It would be deliberate.

***

They were sitting at the table, papers pushed aside, Tess halfway through listing places that felt wrong. Dead ends. Too enclosed. Too many exits. They were thinking off a way to get Daniel to come to them, on their terms, of a way to set a trap.

Perry nodded when it made sense. Shook his head when it didn't. His attention kept slipping, not away from her, but downward, toward the floor, where Otis lay with his head up, eyes open, listening.

Not resting.

Waiting.

Perry noticed it the way he noticed everything now, as a pressure rather than a thought. The room felt tilted, like something was leaning toward him.

He stopped nodding.

"Hold on," he said.

Tess paused. "What?"

Perry didn't answer. He watched Otis instead. Not his face. His body. The tension along his shoulders. The way his tail stayed still but not loose. The way his breathing didn't match the room.

Otis met his eyes.

The sensation that followed wasn't new. It was sharper.

Not an image. Not a sound. Direction.

No.

Perry felt it land, clean and unmistakable. Not refusal, exactly. Correction.

"Okay," Perry said, quietly.

Tess frowned. "Okay what?"

Perry didn't look at her. He kept his eyes on Otis.

"We're wrong about part of it," he said.

Otis shifted, just enough to face the door. Not moving toward it. Marking it.

The pressure came again. Firmer this time.

Not here.
Not like that.

Perry's throat tightened. His first instinct was to pull back, to translate it into something safer. Stress. Projection. Habit.

Then Otis stood.

He walked to the door, stopped short of it, and turned back to Perry. Sat. Waited.

The pressure didn't fade.

Perry swallowed. "You don't want him coming to us," he said.

Otis didn't move.

"You want us going out."

The pressure eased. Not relief. Agreement.

Tess stared at him. "Perry."

"Give me a second," he said.

He crouched, bringing himself level with Otis. He didn't touch him. He didn't need to.

"If we do this," Perry said, carefully, "you stay here."

Otis's ears angled back. The pressure sharpened, quick and hot.

No.

Perry exhaled through his nose. "You don't get a say in this."

The pressure shifted. Not refusal, but negotiation.

"You stay here where you're safe," Perry said.

The pressure thickened. Solid.

Tess's voice came softly now. "Are you---talking to him."

Perry didn't answer right away.

"He wants in it," Perry said. "He insisting."

Otis lay back down, but not the way he had before. Not passive. Ready.

Perry stood slowly. The room felt different now. Not louder. Clearer.

"He wants to help," Perry said. "He's a part of it."

Tess searched his face. "I don't know about this."

Perry looked at Otis. At the calm certainty there, untouched by fear or timing or consequence.

"I don't know either," Perry said.

Otis's eyes stayed on him.

And for the first time since he rescued Otis from the yard, Perry felt something other than pressure.

Disagreement.

Chapter Twenty One - Enough

They didn't talk it through the way people normally do. There was no list. No back and forth. Once the shape of it formed, the details followed without argument.

Perry changed his shoes. Something quieter.

Otis stood in the doorway.

Not waiting. Blocking.

Perry stopped. He looked at him for a moment, then down at the leash hanging by the door.

"No," he said. Not sharp. Not loud. Final.

Otis didn't move.

Tess watched from the kitchen, jacket already on, phone in her hand. She didn't say anything.

"This isn't for you," Perry said.

Otis held his ground. Eyes steady. Body set. Not defiant. Certain.

The pressure wasn't emotional. It wasn't fear. It was simple and direct.

Coming.

Perry exhaled through his nose. "You stay with me," he said. "You don't get ahead of me."

Otis didn't budge.

"You don't chase," Perry said.

Otis stepped back half a pace. Enough to acknowledge. Not enough to retreat.

Perry nodded once.

He picked up the leash and clipped it on. He checked it twice, not for Otis, but for himself. Habit. Control.

Tess pulled on a jacket and checked her phone battery. Then she checked it again. She slid it into her pocket, screen facing her leg, easy to reach.

"I guess it's decided then," she said. "To the mark?"

Perry nodded. He didn't need her to clarify. Daniel's routine didn't shift much. Same window. Same stretch of street.

Otis moved through the door first and stopped just outside, scanning. He waited until Perry stepped out, then fell into place beside him.

Perry closed the door behind them.

They took the longer route. Perry set the pace, turning where he already knew Daniel tended to slow, where he liked to check the street before closing distance. He didn't look back. He didn't need to.

Fewer cars here. Sound carried farther. Perry felt the openness immediately. This was where Daniel usually adjusted his stride.

Otis matched him step for step. No pulling. No lagging.

They walked like that for half a block. Perry felt the familiar urge to move early, to compress the moment.

Otis slowed.

Perry slowed with him.

Otis stopped.

Not abrupt. Not startled.

Perry knew why. This was where Daniel usually lingered before stepping in. Where he waited long enough to feel unseen. They both sensed it.

Perry let the leash slip an inch longer. Not to give Otis space. To acknowledge the timing.

Across the street, Tess crossed without breaking stride and leaned back against a parked car. From where she stood, she had a clear line down the block. Her phone was already in her hand.

Otis didn't look at her.

He stayed forward-facing. Ready.

A car door closed behind them. Too soft. Too controlled.

Otis's ears shifted.

Perry didn't turn.

They were where they needed to be.

Whatever happened next wouldn't start with them.

It would start when Daniel decided he was close enough.

***

Otis sniffed around, as if looking for a spot to pee.

Perry entertained the moment, amused at how well Otis was playing his part.

Perry didn't try to move him along. His abilities were telling him someone was nearing.

Footsteps came up behind them. Unhurried. Close.

"Hey," a man said. "That your dog?"

Perry didn't turn.

"Mind if I pet him?"

Perry already knew who it was. He'd spent hours watching Daniel. The smell confirmed it.

Otis stayed forward-facing, body set.

The space behind Perry tightened.

Daniel stepped around into view and shoved Perry hard in the chest.

Perry rocked back half a step and caught himself.

Daniel stepped in again and grabbed the front of Perry's jacket, fist twisting into fabric. He hauled him forward.

"You thought you could take from me?," Daniel said, breath hot against Perry's face. "You thought I wouldn't notice?"

Perry felt the pressure in the grip, the weight pitched forward.

"Let go!," Perry said.

Daniel's fist tightened. "You don't steal from me and walk away!"

Perry glanced down, just briefly, toward Otis.

"I'll pay you," Perry said. "For the dog. Whatever you want."

Daniel laughed. Sharp. Mean.

"You still don't get it," he said. "It's not about the dog."

He yanked Perry closer.

"It's about respect."

Otis growled.

Low. Immediate.

Daniel's eyes flicked down for the first time.

Otis lunged.

He hit Daniel low, teeth clamping hard at the ankle. Daniel shouted and staggered, grip loosening as he tried to kick free.

"Get the fuck off me!"

Perry twisted out of the hold and stepped back.

Daniel jerked his leg violently, breath tearing out of him as he tried to shake Otis loose.

Otis shifted and bit again, higher this time. Daniel stumbled, balance gone.

Daniel wrenched free with a hard kick and nearly went down. Otis slid back, landed clean, body rigid and ready.

Perry moved between them.

Daniel's face had changed. Control gone. Pain and fury burning through it.

"I'm going to kill you!," Daniel exclaimed.

Perry started away for real.

Otis stayed with him, close.

Across the street, Tess leaned against a parked car. Her phone was already up, held low against her leg, lens steady. The camera Perry had bought for this was running also, clipped to her jacket.

"Stop!," Daniel shouted.

Perry didn't.

Daniel's hand went to his waistband.

The gun came out.

Perry felt the shift before it cleared fabric. The breath drawn and held. The narrowing.

He moved before the trigger finished traveling.

Perry cut left and pulled Otis with him.

The shot cracked the air behind them.

Otis ran.

Perry ran with him.

Daniel fired again.

Perry felt the second pull early and changed direction mid-stride, angling toward the narrow gap between buildings.

Glass shattered. A car alarm screamed. Someone shouted. Doors slammed.

Otis didn't slow until the noise broke apart.

They slipped into a recessed doorway and held there, pressed into shadow.

Otis stayed upright, breathing hard, eyes fixed on the street.

Perry crouched beside him and rested a hand briefly on his collar.

They listened.

Footsteps ran past. Someone yelled something incoherent. A window slammed. The alarm kept going, then cut off.

No one followed.

Perry looked back toward the street.

Daniel was gone.

Across the block, people stood half-exposed in doorways, looking both ways, unsure what they'd just heard. No one moved toward the sound.

The street began to empty itself.

When it felt quiet enough, Perry moved again. Not back the way they'd come. Around the long way, keeping to light, then shadow.

Otis stayed with him, pace steady.

By the time they reached their building, the noise had folded back into the city's usual hum.

Perry unlocked the door. Otis went in first and stopped, listening. Then he moved aside and let Perry follow.

Inside, Perry locked the door and leaned his forehead against it for a moment.

Otis sat nearby, watching him.

Later, Tess let herself in quietly. She closed the door behind her and stood there for a second before moving. She set the phone down carefully, like it might still be recording. She didn't check the footage yet.

That could wait.

The shots existed. The footage existed.

Daniel had crossed a line.

***

They didn't talk at first.

Perry sat on the edge of the couch, shifting his weight, hands opening and closing. The apartment felt smaller than it had that morning. Not threatening. Just aware.

Otis paced once along the length of the room, then stopped near the door and stood there, listening. He wasn't keyed up. Just checking.

Tess moved through the kitchen without turning on the light. She poured a glass of water, took a sip, set it down, then leaned back against the counter.

"You hear anything?" she asked.

Otis's ears shifted. Then settled.

"No," Perry said.

Tess nodded. She reached into her jacket pocket and took out the phone. She didn't unlock it. She just held it for a second, then placed it face down on the table between them.

They all noticed it.

Perry flexed his fingers. The tremor had faded, but the residue hadn't. His body still felt a fraction ahead of the room.

Otis came over and sat near him. Not pressed in. Close enough to register.

"You hurt?" Tess asked.

Perry shook his head. "No."

She looked at Otis.

Otis lifted one paw, set it back down.

Tess exhaled. It slipped out before she caught it.

"He fired, I can't believe he fired," she said.

"I know---I know," Perry said. Still dazed by the events that unfolded.

She nodded. She still didn't touch the phone.

Perry leaned back and closed his eyes for a moment. When he opened them, Otis was watching him. Not searching. Waiting.

"I'm glad he came with us," Perry said.

Tess watched him for a moment, then nodded.

"I didn't stop recording," she said. "Even when I wanted to."

She picked up the phone and unlocked it. The screen lit the room. She watched without sound, jaw set, eyes steady. When it ended, she locked it again and set it down.

"That's not ambiguous," she said.

"No," Perry said.

Otis stood and moved to the window. He didn't look out. He just stood near it, back to the room.

Perry tracked the movement without turning his head.

"He may disappear for a while now," Tess said. "But not forever."

Perry nodded.

The apartment shifted into a different quiet. Not the brittle kind from before. Something flatter. Real.

Otis turned and lay down, head on his paws, eyes still open.

Perry let his shoulders drop.

Outside, a car passed. Somewhere farther away, someone laughed.

The world kept going. It just felt closer now.

Chapter Twenty Two – Still Here

Morning didn't change the situation.

It only made the apartment visible again.

Perry stood at the kitchen window, watching the street without focusing on it. His bag sat open on the table behind him, half-packed. It had been like that for days. A reminder, not a decision.

Otis lay near the doorway, awake. Not resting. Tracking.

Tess moved quietly, keeping her movements economical. She set a mug down near Perry's hand. He didn't touch it.

"They can see everything," she said.

Perry nodded.

"Faces," she continued. "Yours. His. Clear enough that there's no question."

"That was the point," Perry said.

She studied him, then nodded once.

Otis stood and came over, stopping close to Perry's leg. He didn't look outside. He watched Perry.

"We don't attach ourselves to it," Tess said. "It goes in clean."

Perry nodded. "Like an anonymous bystander."

"Yes," Tess said. "Someone who happened to be there."

She reached into her pocket and set the USB drive on the table. It made a dulled sound when it landed.

"They'll still come to you," she said.

"Yes," Perry said. "But not to you."

Otis's ears shifted.

"Not yet," Perry said.

Otis stayed where he was.

"This was always the trade," Tess said.

Perry nodded.

"When he's in custody," she said.

"Then I go," Perry said.

"And if he isn't?"

"Then I stay," Perry said. "We don't leave it loose."

Tess watched him for a moment. "And the woman?"

Perry nodded. "She's still part of it."

Tess didn't hesitate. "If he feels cornered, he goes home, I'm worried for her."

Perry nodded once. "That's why this has to move."

The silence that followed wasn't fear. It was agreement.

"If he's smart," Tess said, "he disappears."

"He isn't," Perry said.

"And if he panics?"

"Then he moves fast," Perry said. "And ugly."

Otis shifted, unsettled but present.

"We submit it today," Perry said.

Tess picked up the drive and slid it into a padded envelope. She sealed it carefully, methodical.

"No return," she said.

"No trail," Perry said.

She slipped the envelope into her bag.

"I'll take care of it," she said.

Perry nodded.

Outside, a truck idled, then pulled away. A door opened somewhere down the block. Someone laughed. Ordinary sounds, still allowed to exist.

Perry closed his bag, then pushed it back under the table.

A week was still a week.

But now it mattered.

***

Perry went alone.

The precinct was quieter than he expected. Midday. Fluorescent lights. A low, steady hum that made everything feel slightly unreal.

He stood at the counter for a moment before anyone noticed him.

"I need to report an incident," he said.

The officer looked up, took him in, then nodded toward a chair. "Someone will be with you."

Perry sat. His leg bounced once before he stopped it.

A few minutes later, an officer came out and gestured toward a small room off the side hall.

Inside, there was a table, two chairs, and a camera mounted high in one corner. It wasn't pointed directly at him. It didn't need to be.

"What happened?," the officer said.

Perry took a breath. He didn't rush it.

"I was threatened," he said. "Last night. A man approached me on the street while I was walking my dog."

Perry nodded. "I found him a few weeks ago. No collar. No chip."

The officer wrote, unremarkable, just recording.

"He started talking to me," Perry continued. "At first it didn't seem aggressive. He asked if he could pet the dog. Then he got close."

"How close?," the officer said.

"Too close," Perry said. "He shoved me. Grabbed my jacket."

The pen paused.

"What was he saying?"

Perry looked at the table, then back up.

"He said I stole his dog," Perry said. "Kept repeating it."

"And you?"

"I told him I found the dog, I think," Perry said. "That I didn't know him. I said I'd pay him because I was scared and wanted to get away."

The officer's pen moved again.

"How did he respond?"

"He laughed," Perry said. "Said it wasn't about the dog anymore. Said I'd taken something from him."

Perry continued, steady. "Then he started talking about respect. About teaching me a lesson."

The officer glanced up briefly, then back down.

"Then what?"

"He pulled a gun," Perry said. "Pointed it at me. Told me to stop."

"You didn't."

"I didn't," Perry said. "I ran."

"He fired."

"Yes."

"How many times?"

"Twice," Perry said. "I didn't look back."

The officer leaned back slightly.

"Was anyone hurt?"

"No, I don't believe so," Perry said. "He missed."

"When did this happen?"

Perry gave the time.

"And you're reporting it now."

"Yes."

"Why the delay?"

Perry didn't hedge.

"I was afraid," he said. "I didn't know if he'd follow me. I didn't know if coming here right away would make things worse."

The officer watched him for a moment, then nodded and continued writing.

"Anyone else with you?"

"No."

"Witnesses?"

"I don't know," Perry said. "There might've been people around."

The officer tapped the pen once, then closed the notebook partway.

"We may have received some material related to this incident," he said. "We're still reviewing it."

Perry looked up. "What kind of material."

"Video," the officer said. Neutral. "Possibly from a bystander."

Perry absorbed that. He nodded once.

"Wow, Okay," he said.

"We'll follow up," the officer said. "Don't leave town."

Perry met his eyes. "I won't."

Outside, the air felt heavier. Not dangerous. Just solid.

Perry stood on the steps for a moment, then moved.

He didn't call Tess.

He walked home.

Otis was waiting by the door when he came in. Not excited. Just present.

Perry closed the door and rested his hand briefly on Otis's head.

"One step," he said.

It wasn't relief. But it was movement.

Chapter Twenty Three - Different

Perry stepped out of the precinct. Traffic moved through the intersection. A bus pulled away from the curb. Someone laughed nearby.

He stopped on the sidewalk and listened. Nothing stood out.

His phone buzzed.

Tess: I'm home with Otis.

Perry typed back: On my way.

He walked. Not the shortest route. The one with more turns. More places to stop if he needed to.

Sounds separated as he moved. Tires on asphalt. Footsteps behind him, then past him. A radio through an open window. Smells came and went without pattern. Nothing held his attention longer than it should have.

At the building, he paused at the door and listened again.

Nothing.

Inside, the stairwell hummed. He climbed without rushing. Before he reached the landing, Otis's nails clicked once on the other side of the door.

Tess opened it before he knocked.

Otis stood behind her, ears forward, body loose. Watching.

Perry stepped inside and locked the door. Then checked it.

"You okay?" Tess said.

"Yeah."

She handed him a glass of water. He drank it.

"They took it seriously," she said.

"They did, they mentioned receiving something they thought could be related"

Otis moved closer and sat beside him. Perry crouched and rested a forearm along the dog's back. Otis stayed still.

"I don't like waiting," Perry said.

"I know," Tess said. "But this part isn't yours."

"They said don't leave town" Perry said.

"Did you mention Canada?" Tess asked.

"No," Perry replied.

A car door slammed outside. Otis's ears shifted, then relaxed.

Perry crossed to the window and looked out. The street was the same as it had been earlier.

"He doesn't know where we are," Perry said.

"Not yet," Tess said.

"For as long as that holds," Perry said.

She nodded.

They stood there. Otis stayed near them, facing the room.

Elsewhere, things were moving. Paperwork. Calls. Decisions. None of it had reached them.

For now, they stayed where they were.

***

They had been inside for two days.

Curtains half drawn. Lights kept low. Otis was walked early and late. The walks were brief. No one lingered longer than they had to.

Waiting filled the apartment.

Perry marked time by ordinary sounds. The refrigerator cycling on. A car backing up somewhere nearby. Otis shifting position near the door.

Canada sat just ahead of him. Two days. A flight. A role he could hardly afford to miss.

That afternoon, Perry stood near the window with his phone pressed to his ear.

"I start rehearsals right away," he said. "They want me there early."

His mother's voice came through steady and familiar.

"That's good," she said. "You sound tired."

"I'm fine," Perry said. "No need to worry."

His phone buzzed in his hand. Another call coming in.

Rina.

Perry glanced at the name, then looked back out the window. He didn't want to break the call. He didn't want questions. He let it ring.

It stopped.

A second later, the phone buzzed again with a voicemail notification.

He didn't check it. He'd do that later.

Rina had been opening the shop.

The gate had been halfway up. The lights had still been off. She had been alone.

Daniel had stepped inside and stood between her and the door.

"Where is he?," Daniel had said.

She had seen the gun before he finished the question.

Rina had told him what she knew. That Perry was staying with his girlfriend. That it was an apartment building she knew by name. She hadn't known the unit. She hadn't known the floor. She had said it fast because he promised to return if she lied to him, and she wanted him gone.

Daniel had turned and left.

Rina had locked the door with shaking hands and called the police. She had told them about the gun. About the threat. About the building Daniel said he was going to. It had been enough to give them direction.

She had called Perry next.

He hadn't answered.

Rina had stayed on the line. She had spoken quickly. Said his name more than once. Said there was no time.

Perry never heard it.

Back at the apartment, Perry stopped mid-sentence.

Something had shifted.

Not sound. Not movement. Presence. A smell that didn't belong to the building. Sweat gone sour. No caution left in it.

"Perry?" his mother said.

"He's here," Perry said quietly.

Tess was already standing. She didn't ask who.

Perry ended the call. "Now."

They moved without panic. Tess grabbed her jacket. Perry clipped the leash. Otis stayed tight to his leg.

Boots hit the stairs. Fast. Heavy. Coming up.

The doorknob rattled once.

Then the door broke inward.

They were already out the window.

The fire escape shook as they climbed down. Otis took the ladder first. Perry followed, then Tess.

Above them, Daniel's voice tore through the apartment, furious at finding it empty.

He turned and ran for the stairs.

Out front, patrol cars were already turning onto the block. Sirens cut off as they slid into place. Doors opened. Commands overlapped.

Daniel burst through the front door and stopped.

There was nowhere left.

"Hands!" someone shouted.

He tried anyway. He didn't get far.

From the alley, Perry watched Daniel driven to the pavement. Cuffs closed. Someone read from a card. Someone else kept a knee planted until it was done.

The pressure eased, slowly.

Tess's hand was tight around Perry's wrist. Otis stood pressed against his leg, steady.

"Let's go," Tess said.

They didn't wait to be seen.

They moved deeper into the block, away from the lights and the noise.

Two days left.

Chapter Twenty Four - Now

They slept that night.

Not deeply. Not all at once. But enough.

Morning came through the curtains in pieces. Perry woke first. Otis was already awake, watching the door, tail still.

Tess's phone buzzed on the table.

She checked it, then sat up.

"He's in," she said.

Perry waited.

"Holding him without bail. Gun charges. Assault. Attempted murder." She let out a breath she hadn't finished taking the night before. "They're saying trial, not a deal."

"Good," Perry said.

"They don't expect him out."

Otis shifted closer.

Later, Perry took the subway across town.

The woman's place smelled different now. Windows open. Air moving through. She didn't invite him in right away. She stood in the doorway, arms crossed, eyes moving past him to the street.

"They said he can't come near me," she said.

"He won't," Perry said.

She nodded, but didn't step aside.

Perry stayed anyway. Not long. Long enough.

They talked about practical things. What needed fixing. Who she'd called. Who she hadn't. He helped move a chair back where it belonged. Wrote down a number she kept losing.

"You don't have to stay," she said.

"I know," Perry said.

He left when she was ready, not when the conversation ran out.

Back at the apartment, Tess was packing.

Not everything. Just enough to clear space.

"The detective said they'll probably need you," she said. "For the trial."

"I figured," Perry said.

"But not right away."

"No, they haven't set a date yet."

They sat on the floor with Otis between them.

"You still going?," Tess asked.

"Yes."

She nodded. Didn't look away.

"I'll come back," Perry said.

"I know," she said.

Otis lifted his head, then settled again, like the decision had already been made.

That night, Perry finished packing.

One bag. The same one he'd used before.

Tess watched from the bed. Didn't offer help. Didn't leave the room.

"You ready?," she asked.

"Yes."

She stood and kissed him. Slow. Certain.

"Go," she said. "Do us proud."

"I will."

Otis stood between them, tail low, watching both faces.

"We're three now," Tess said.

Perry smiled.

"Yes," he said.

Tomorrow, he would leave.

Nothing was pulling at him anymore.

Otis

You were a lover,

a brave defender, always alert.

Small only in stature,

electric with life.

Rattled by thunder,

warm and generous.

A cuddler.

Ever present.

Something to look forward to

at the end of the day.

Unwavering.

Funny.

Unique.

Finicky in ways only you could be.

Irreplaceable.

Family.

Rest now.

www.ingramcontent.com/pod-product-compliance
Lightning Source LLC
Chambersburg PA
CBHW020153120726
47903CB00007B/2541